Cooper.
Happy Birthday!
Best Wishes

GIONNE

CHRIS DALE

Copyright © First published in Great Britain

October 2024

Copyright © 2021 Chris Dale

The moral right of Christopher Dale to be identified as the author of this work has been asserted in accordance with the Copyright, Designs and Patents Act 1988.

All rights reserved. No part of this publication may be reproduced or transmitted in any form or by any means, electronic or mechanical including photocopy, recording or any information storage and retrieval system, without the permission in writing of the author and from the publisher.

This book is a work of fiction. All the characters, names, businesses, organisations, some of the places and events in this story are fictitious and the product of the author's wild imagination. Any resemblance to actual persons, living or dead, or events is entirely coincidental!

DEDICATION

To Siân, in memory of Gionne her magnificent black, Friesian.

And also to Mike Landrey for his invaluable advice and experience on everything Dutch.

ACKNOWLEDGEMENTS

This is my 15th book. I was inspired to write it after a conversation with a good friend who had a magnificent, black horse named Gionne, a Friesian from Holland. It immediately sparked my interest, and the rest is here for you to read.

I have been most fortunate to have the help of my good friend Mike Landrey, who has extensive knowledge of Holland and the Dutch language, having lived there. He has guided me in both terminology and how people lived in the 18th century. I have tried to keep to original Dutch words, for instance the word for Mr, Sir or man is *Meneer* and a married woman is *Vrouw*. Research on 18th-century Friesland (known as Frisia) is sparse, and although most of the geography and townships existed, some I have made up, including Franeker. Girls went to dame schools, whereas boys went to academy schools and were taught different subjects. Religion has always been difficult to write about, especially as there were religious divisions in Holland at the time. I apologise if anything written herein does not seem entirely accurate to you, the reader, but it's close to how things would have been at the time.

The story will take us to England, and I have taken the liberty of using both a family and area of the Lincolnshire

Wolds from my book, *When Her Head Hits the Pillow*. I've used these as I live in the county and am familiar with the area. I've also used the fictitious county of Flintshire, in England. The characters from this book are obviously 3rd or 4th generation, as the story in my other book was based in the 17th century, but they lend themselves to this book as well.

My thanks also go to John Kain who tirelessly proofreads my books for me. Also, to Amanda Jacobs (AJ), who edits the storyline and grammar and ensures it makes sense, as well as to my team of beta readers, including Anita Bolton and Laura Middleton, who give me an indication of the book's realism.

The final edit was made possible with immense help from Susie Ryder, who shaped up the storyline and created a tighter, more polished read. Susie is a professional editor and can be contacted on susiejryder@gmail.com and to Nathan Ryder who designed the book cover.

CHARACTERS

Gionne van't Kroenraedt

Janus van't Kroenraedt – Gionne's father

Lenje van't Kroenraedt – Gionne's mother

Pim de Vries

Truus de Vries – Pim's younger sister

Pieter de Vries – Pim's father

Maritje de Vries – Pim's mother

Maarten de Vries – Pim's uncle in the port of Delfzijl

Karen de Vries – Pim's aunt, wife of Maarten

Joost and Casper de Vries – Maarten and Karen's sons

Willem Janseen – Ship's Master

Jacob van de Cloos – Trader at port of Delzijl

Jaap Boerhuis – Odious, rotund port dweller

Her Pedersen – Wealthy landowner

Commissioner Johan Hendricks – Dutch Army, covering crime

Major General Albert Leijtens – overall commander of the Dutch Army in the region and father of Hans Leijtens

Captain Hans Leijtens – Senior ranking officer, reporting to Commissioner Hendricks

Lieutenant Carl Leijtens – officer under Hans Leijtens, his cousin. Nephew of Major General Albert Leijtens

Lord Henry Bankes - 5th Marquis of Flintshire

Lady Harrietta Bankes – Marchioness of Flintshire (was Harrietta de Vries, Pieter's sister)

Claude Smithy – Boatman, Hull

General Clifford Stanley – High Sheriff of Flintshire

Sir Bernard Failsworth – Earl of Corringham

Lady Louise Failsworth – Viscountess of Corringham

Randulph Blake – Estate Steward

James Howell – Head Butler

Mrs Cribb – Head Housekeeper

Mrs Pottage – Head Cook

George Bedlan – First Footman

Tobias Tilley III – Gamekeeper

Anouk – Gionne's Friesian horse

Bea – Gionne's Keeshond dog and Viggo- Pim's horse

PROLOGUE
1758

The year is 1758 and William V had been on the throne as King of the Dutch Republic for just over ten years. The landed nobility had relatively little importance as influencers, since they mostly lived in the more underdeveloped inland provinces. It was the urban merchant class that dominated Dutch society. Social status was largely determined by income.

It was on the 19th May that year that Lenje van't Koenraedt delivered a baby girl in the front room of their farmhouse, with a midwife and the help of her husband Janus. The couple were overjoyed as they had been trying for some considerable time, having been married nearly fourteen years. Both were already into their early thirties, and they had almost given up hope of having a family.

'We shall name her Gionne,' announced Janus proudly to everyone's surprise.

Obedient as always, Lenje complied with the decision made by her husband and got on with nursing her new baby girl.

Their farm was in the middle of nowhere in the flatlands of Friesland in the north of the Dutch Republic. The nearest village, Franeker, was ten kilometres away; their main town, Leeuwarden, a good half day on horseback. They owned several horses, but the horses were mainly used for working in the fields, pulling ploughs and other farm machinery.

Growing mainly vegetables to supply the Dutch East India Company sailing vessels to feed the crews, as well as flowers for the landed gentry, Janus and Lenje lived and worked the farm that had been in Janus's family for three generations.

Considered wealthy by most, Janus had a position in society as well as the local governing body and was widely respected as an honest and trustworthy man.

Janus and Lenje became strict parents; they'd both had a Dutch Catholic upbringing – the main religion there at that time. Every Sunday, they both attended the local church, which was run by a Jesuit priest in the next village.

The couple wanted more children but sadly, Lenje had suffered several miscarriages and was advised not to try again after Gionne was born. Subsequently, they tended to wrap her in cotton wool.

Although shielded from the outside world in their rural community, the country was in turmoil after decades of rigid conservatism by the Princes of Orange. The young William V was in an alliance with England, whilst courting both the French and the Russians, developing the Dutch Republic into the Netherlands.

More upheaval was to come in the Anglo-Dutch war that impacted on trade and the produce from the farm.

♦♦♦

Gionne's tuition was home-based, mostly by her mother and their local priest who gave her religious education, as the nearest school was too far away to travel every day.

She was taught to read and write in North Frisian, the local language that was similar to German. In addition, she was also taught Dutch and English as Lenje could foresee a time when a spoken knowledge of the main languages would be beneficial to her. Gionne had a natural ear and vocabulary, making her an excellent pupil in all three languages.

As Gionne grew up, Lenje gave her some housework duties, and she would supervise the field workers and prepare their food for lunch and dinner.

However, Gionne preferred to work out in the fields with her father or in the stables and developed a closer relationship with him than with her mother. Her duties on the farm included her favourite: looking after the horses.

Janus doted on his daughter and taught her everything about farming, including ploughing sowing seeds, animal husbandry, and even how to work the foundry to repair the farm equipment, horseshoes and tackle.

Her mother sometimes despaired of her daughter becoming too much of a tomboy and not learning the skills of housekeeping, cooking, sewing and general cleanliness in the house.

At the age of fourteen in 1772, Gionne's thirst for knowledge was pushing her mother and the priest beyond their capabilities and her parents reluctantly enrolled her in the new dame school that had recently opened in the nearest village. To enable her to attend this school, her father bought her a beautiful, black Friesian mare, which she named Anouk, so she could ride to attend classes.

She regarded Anouk as her horse, although it still had to earn its keep by working on the farm, pulling ploughs and carts, when Gionne was not at school. Occasionally, when her home chores were completed, she was allowed to ride out on Anouk as long as she was back by sunset.

CHAPTER ONE
The Early Years

At 16 years of age, Gionne was suddenly discovering there was a world that existed outside of her home on the farm in Friesland, and that her parents had been cocooning her from the realities of life.

As dame school in Leeuwarden was quite a distance from home, Gionne was a week border, going home only at weekends. She quickly became popular as her knowledge and intelligence was way ahead of the other girls, thanks to the very solid grounding given to her by her mother and the priest. In terms of character, she was always polite, and she listened to others before she gave an opinion which was never conceited or condescending. She rapidly became the teachers' favourite, helping other girls who were not as gifted as her.

Gionne formed friendships with a few girls her age. One was Truus de Vries, and Gionne considered Truus her best friend. Her family were landed gentry, her father being the local Baron. Truus had a brother, Pim, who was a year older and went to the boys' academe in Leeuwarden. Gionne would see Pim each afternoon after dame school, when she came to meet Truus to escort her to the boarding home, and that was the start of their relationship.

Despite an awkward, bumbling, shy start, they became good friends. Gionne was a tomboy and Pim made the perfect sparring partner.

Truus began to get jealous of her best friend's bond with her brother.

♦♦♦

Gionne felt a spark of excitement every time she saw Pim and, when he looked at her, she had a rush of blood to her head.

She was confused; her home education had not included matters of the heart or any type of sex education, as her parents were very strict about that sort of thing. Her body was also changing, and she couldn't understand what was happening to her.

One day, at the start of the school holidays, Truus invited Gionne to her home to meet her parents.

'Please Mama,' she asked her mother, 'the de Vries are a very noble family, and I want to meet them. It will only be for a few days after school.'

'We will have to ask your father's permission first. He has dealings with de Vries, who buys our produce, and he goes to town meetings with him.'

That evening after supper, it became clear her father was totally against the idea, and he said no, firmly. Gionne heard her mother suggesting that it would be good for their daughter to experience how other families lived – after all, the de Vries family were very upstanding members of their small community. Her father, however, was unrelenting.

'But they are not of our religion, and I don't want our daughter's head filled with their ideas!'

'Our daughter is very bright, Janus. We cannot hold her back now that she has gone to the dame school. Her education will only grow stronger if we expose her to the wider world. We should show a little trust in her and let her spread her wings a little.'

'I don't know. I am not happy with her head being filled with the ideas of de Vries and his kin,' he said.

'She is a strong-willed girl and if we impose too tight a rein on her, she will rebel at some time. Why not let her experience this whilst we can still control her?' her mother implored.

At this point, neither her mother nor her father knew anything about Pim or the feelings Gionne had when in his company.

'Let me sleep on it,' Janus said.

Gionne heard their conversation through the loose floorboards in her attic bedroom of their old farmhouse.

She grinned with delight. It was the first time she had ever heard her father falter on a decision!

She loved her mother even more for fighting her case. That night she could not sleep.

Gionne was up early the next morning. It was a cold and wet start to the day, but this did not change her mood. She went to the well and drew out a bucket of water to fill the giant kettles on the stove in the kitchen so everyone could wash and have a warm drink.

Then she went about her morning chores: feeding the chickens, getting Anouk and the working horses into the stable from the field and brushing them down with straw to dry them as much as she could, knowing they would soon be going back out to work the fields.

Janus stood in the huge barn doorway watching his beloved daughter work so lovingly with the horses. He knew she had been up for a good few hours and had dutifully completed all her chores. He was proud of her and saw what a beautiful young lady she was becoming. She reminded him of Lenje when he had first met her. Lenje had been slightly older than Gionne was now – around 17. He remembered how he had felt: his heart pounding in his chest, his head filled with admiration for her, not being able to take his eyes off her when they met. He was shy, inexperienced at how to talk to the opposite sex, especially someone he liked. He also wondered how his parents would feel if he asked to be formally betrothed to her, as was the custom within his community. Thankfully, her parents were in the same religious sect as his family. He knew his wife was right. Gionne was a very bright, strong-willed young lady and nothing seemed to faze her.

Looking at his daughter now, and totally against his initial instincts, he made up his mind. He hoped he would not regret it.

'Gionne!' He greeted her with a kiss on her forehead.

'Father, good morning,' she said politely.

'Your mother has spoken to me about the invitation you have received to go to the de Vries' with their daughter Truus.'

'Yes,' she said, her hopes rising.

'Well, I've thought about it, and I will allow you to go. However, you must promise to say your prayers and be very polite.'

Gionne flung herself into his arms with delight and hugged her father.

'Thank you, thank you, thank you, Papa!'

She squealed in delight and ran to see her mother.

Janus watched his beautiful daughter, skirt tails in hand, skipping into the farmhouse, singing and elated. He was suddenly sad at the prospect that he was about to lose his precious child.

♦♦♦

A vagrant was walking along the riverbank, just a few kilometres from the van't Kroenraedt farm. It was a cold; wet morning and the low mist had turned into a constant drizzle. He pulled his heavy sheepskin coat over his head and continued his journey. He was hoping for some work from the

Dutch farmer in return for food and perhaps somewhere warm and dry to sleep the night.

He initially felt the earth vibrate before he heard the deep, rhythmic beating of hooves from a horse galloping at speed and approaching through the mist behind him.

He never felt the long, thin steel blade as it penetrated through his sheepskin coat, sank between his shoulder blades and pierced his heart.

He crumpled to the ground and rolled into the gully of the river as the horse and rider sped past.

His body remained there for several weeks before a passer-by spotted him and reported it to the town hall in the next village.

CHAPTER TWO
The Aristocrats

A month later, Gionne stepped into a fine carriage with Truus and Pim as they were collected from outside dame school. A uniformed footman took her carpetbag and placed it on the roof with the rest of the bags, then a pair of fine horses pulled the carriage away and towards the de Vries estate, about an hour's ride away.

The carriage turned through an arched stone gateway with a gold-leafed coat of arms centred on the top of the arch. Black iron gates stood open, and the small gatehouse appeared empty. Gionne gazed at the long straight drive that bordered open parkland and led to the de Vries country estate. The house was a huge, all white, two-storey building built of stone, with very tall windows on the ground floor and smaller windows directly above. These windows were made up of small square glass panels. There were three on each side with an extended wing of the house at each end. The roof was grey Dutch tile with tall brick chimneys reaching up. At the front of the roof a large clock was built into a bell tower. The house looked amazing.

Gionne's mouth felt open as she gazed at the extent of the building unfolding as they neared. Tall trees surrounded the house on either side and beautifully manicured gardens, edged with finely cut privet hedges, spread out in front of it. A broad sweep of gravel welcomed them.

The carriage pulled up in front of a pillared front entrance. Tall black oak doors opened, and the house staff formed a semi-circle behind someone Gionne assumed was Truus and Pim's mother – a tall, elegantly-dressed lady with an air about her that breathed class and social standing.

Gionne was slightly nervous about meeting her. It was clear from where Truus and Pim got their looks; she was not just elegant, but beautiful, too.

Truus and Pim were both very excited that they had a guest for the weekend, Pim especially as he really liked Gionne. They jumped out of the carriage and rushed to embrace their mother as Gionne gingerly stepped down onto the gravel and walked slowly, head bowed, towards her.

'Mamma … may I present our new friend, Gionne van't Koenraedt.'

Gionne took the outstretched hand, gave a small curtsy and lightly brushed her lips on the white-gloved hand.

'I am delighted to meet you, Madam de Vries, and thank you for inviting me to your home,' she said politely. Gionne had no idea there was more to the invite than met the eye.

At 17 years old, Pim was finishing at the academe and needed to seek a trade. His father wanted him to experience another job before he entered the family business in Amsterdam. As Pieter and Janus were acquainted, there was an ulterior motive behind Gionne's invitation: Pieter had the idea that his son should work for Janus to learn traditional farming methods and build experience to manage their own estate.

The de Vries were wealthy and the fourth generation of a traditional Dutch family. They owned shipping companies in Antwerp and Rotterdam, were extensive landowners dockside and had a very profitable business based in Amsterdam, importing precious stones to turn into jewellery to trade. Pieter and Maritje de Vries had open minds about religion and politics and supported whichever party would benefit their business empire the most.

Very quickly, Gionne became popular with both the de Vries family as well as the household staff. Her natural kind, demeanour and her quick mind impressed all who met her.

Being members of the nobility, the de Vries were close to the royal family and the upper circle. Truus and Pim were used to the court formalities, rituals and pleasantries. They soon realised that

Gionne would be out of her depth at some of the evening and lunch parties the family had been invited to attend.

Truus had flagged this up with her mother, who planned to dress Gionne appropriately and – together with Truus and their chief housemaid – educate her out of her country ways.

And so, the 16-year-old Gionne learnt how to become a lady.

She loved it: the high-fashion dresses made of fine silks and cottons with layers of undergarments she had never experienced before. Maritje and Truus laughed at Gionne's expressions when the manicurists and hairdressers started her transformation from farm girl to lady.

She quickly learnt deportment, etiquette, table manners, and her social education continued with the refined culture, the food, and the circle of aristocracy to whom she was going to be introduced.

Pim was at her side for every function, day or night. He didn't allow any male suitors to present themselves to her. Truus found this amusing and teased her brother about his growing infatuation with Gionne.

Pim was totally unaware that he was falling in love with Gionne, although everyone around them could see it.

Pieter sent Janus a message requesting that their daughter be allowed to stay for the entire school holiday as she was becoming very popular with all their friends. He added that they were impressed by her discipline in her daily prayers and that she had become an ardent reader in their library.

♦♦♦

The messenger was asked to wait for a reply at the farm.

At first, Janus was totally against his daughter being indoctrinated into the de Vries way of life, fearful her education was being affected.

'This is what I feared, Lenje. Her head will be filled with all their nonsense, and she will develop aspirations in life we cannot afford to give her!'

He paused to light his pipe, puffing smoke out as the tobacco embers glowed with each strong pull of air.

'No … I am against this,' he said firmly.

Lenje was always influential in persuading Janus what would be best for their daughter.

'Janus, you are a good and caring man, and our only daughter is precious to both of us. But if we hold her back, she may rebel, and we both want her to have the best start in life possible. The de Vries are a good family with high family values. Gionne has a good head on her shoulders, and I have every confidence in her. Let her have this opportunity to see another side of life.'

'There is an ulterior motive. I am convinced de Vries is after something from us, otherwise why spend time and money on our daughter?'

Eventually, the messenger left with his answer.

♦♦♦

They were in the games room playing cards, as Gionne waited in anticipation. She feared her father would put his foot down and refuse her an extension to her time with Pim and Truus. Her mood was sombre and no amount of light-hearted chatter from Truus would lift her gloom. Pim was aware of her thoughts, and he too was downhearted at the prospect of seeing her return home. He realised that she meant more to him than he'd thought.

The door of the games room squeaked open and in strode a bustling and very merry Maritje de Vries.

'Come you three, you all look as if it's the end of the world!' She had a wide smile as she stood in front of them, hands on hips.

'Mamma ... you have news for us. The messenger that just arrived ... we saw him,' Truus probed.

Maritje smiled and swung around to make the frills on her dress twirl, keeping them in suspense.

All three sat on a chaise longue in front of her, their faces awash with expectant looks.

'Your father has agreed to your extended stay, Gionne … with certain conditions.'

The initial elation on hearing the news swiftly turned into a groan as Gionne raised her head to hear what conditions her father had imposed.

'What do I have to do?' she asked petulantly.

'Nothing that you are not already doing, young lady. You are a credit to your parents and a good influence on Truus and Pim.'

That evening, after supper, Gionne went to explore the stable block with the idea of taking a horse for a ride. Pim watched her leave and decided to follow her at a discreet distance. He was fascinated by her and watched as she gathered up her dress, revealing what looked like gentleman's jodhpurs or culottes beneath. She ran into the stable yard.

Pim watched her peering into each stable block until she found what she was looking for and disappeared within.

A few minutes later the stable door was pushed open. Gionne sat bareback, hugging the horse's neck to lower her profile to anyone watching and trotted out of the yard and into the field beyond.

Pim was curious and concerned at the same time. For Gionne to ride out at night bareback into unfamiliar countryside was not only dangerous but foolish.

He walked to his horse's stable and quickly strapped on a hunting saddle and bridle, before jumping into the saddle and galloping after her.

He decided to keep a safe distance back to see where she was going and rode on the parkland to quieten down the sound of his horse's hooves.

There was a full moon and he soon spied her in the distance. She was cantering towards the stone archway entrance, where she turned onto the main road leading to the local village.

He continued to follow at a distance. The gatehouse door opened and the gateman took his long pipe out of his mouth and doffed his cap at

Pim. He said nothing – just retreated into his warm cottage as Pim trotted past.

Pim watched as Gionne slowed her horse to a walk near the village. Just at the perimeter, she jumped off and tethered her horse to a post. Pim was now very worried about her; what was she doing here? After all, she knew no one from this small farming village. Or did she? Was there a relative who lived here? If so, why not tell Truus or him about them? Was she embarrassed because they would be in the de Vries employment?

He stopped his mount short of the outskirts and dismounted. His horse bent to eat grass.

Pim walked quietly into the village, hugging the walls and keeping under the darkest cover he could find.

She had disappeared.

Pim stalked the full length of the main street. There were candles burning in some of the houses, but in the main it was deserted. He could not see where she had gone or even if she was in the village.

After an hour of this skulking under cover or behind walls, there was no sign of Gionne, so Pim made his way back to his horse only find hers had gone.

As he entered the stable block, he could see the door for her horse was closed. He dismounted and led his horse inside, took off the saddle and bridle, and fed it some oats.

Pim made his way back into the house, removed his riding boots and walked in socks up the back staircase along the corridor to the guest wing.

Gionne's bedroom door was closed and he heard nothing from within.

The next morning, Gionne was at breakfast looking radiant and happy as Pim walked in.

'Good morning, Mamma, good morning, dearest sister and good morning my dear Gionne. And may I say how beautiful and radiant you look this morning, after your busy night?'

Gionne glowered at him, a frown sullying her usually perfect forehead.

'I'm sorry. I don't understand what you mean, Pim. Please explain.'

'I thought I saw you taking a moonlit ride last night,' he said, casually pouring a cup of coffee.

'You must mistake me for one of your other admirers for I slept extremely well all night.' Gionne's gaze never left his face.

'Pim, please! How dare you make such accusations!' declared Truus.

'Yes,' said Maritje de Vries, 'you must mind your manners. Gionne is a special guest, and you must not tease her so.'

'Oh, I am not mistaken. And it's nice to know *you* are one of my admirers,' he said with a wink and a smile.

Pieter de Vries walked into the breakfast room, and they all stood up, even his wife. He took his chair at the head of the table and one of the breakfast maids brought him coffee and his usual.

'What was all that commotion, young master Pim?' he asked of his youngest son.

'Nothing, Pater. Just teasing our guest of honour,' he said defiantly.

'We have brought you up to have better manners. I do apologise on behalf of my wayward son, Miss van't Koenraedt,' he said in his deep voice.

'No matter Her de Vries, and please call me Gionne. I am unaccustomed to such formality,' she said, slightly embarrassed.

'I do hope you are enjoying your stay with us Gionne and that Truus and this young whippersnapper are looking after you.'

'I have indeed learned so much from your family, Her de Vries. You have a wonderful house and gardens, so different from our humble farm,' she said unafraid to speak out.

'Yes … your father runs a very good farm, I hear, and it would be good for Pim to learn the basics in agriculture. I must speak with Janus at some stage,' he added.

So that's why I was invited to stay longer, Gionne thought: *as a sort of exchange.* She remembered overhearing her father's comment to her mother; he'd suspected Pieter de Vries would want something in return.

After breakfast, Gionne, Truus and Pim had academic lessons in the grand hall, followed by deportment and etiquette lessons in the afternoon.

Pim was desperate to get Gionne on his own to ask her about last night but with a packed programme of events, dinners and other social engagements over the next week, they were scarcely alone.

Towards the end of that week, the body of a traveller was discovered under the rotting cover of a disused cart at the back of the village barn. News of this reached the de Vries family late that night when the village elder came to present himself to his landlord Pieter de Vries.

Pim remembered he had looked inside the barn the night he followed Gionne and noticed the old cart. She had spent some time in there as he waited outside.

Surely not …

CHAPTER THREE
6 weeks later

Pim realised that he was falling in love with Gionne. The more time he spent with her, the more he wanted to be with her, and she was not shy with demonstrating her feelings for him either, flirting at every possible moment.

Pim had pushed his suspicions about Gionne to the back of his mind and soon forgot about the vagrant in the barn.

Truus was becoming increasingly aware of the growing bond between her brother and her best friend but she had very mixed feelings. On the one hand, she didn't know what to think or say, so just pretended it wasn't happening; on the other, she was becoming jealous of both her brother and her best friend.

◆◆◆

And so, the time finally came when Gionne had to return to her home in Northern Friesland and to normality.

The whole de Vries family came out to see her off.

Pieter shook her hand formally with a smile, whilst Maritje gave her a tight hug, whispering, 'You will always be welcome here anytime – you know that.' She gave Gionne a kiss on the forehead.

Truus was in tears and didn't want her to go, pleading to her mother and father to let her stay longer.

'We shall all see Gionne again soon – maybe after the next academic term,' her father said.

Pim took both of her gloved hands into his and kissed her on both cheeks.

'We will see each other soon,' he said in a lowered voice. 'You'll see.'

Gionne was very sad on her long journey back by carriage, her mind recalling all the wonderful experiences she had with the de Vries family.

She was looking forward to seeing her mother and father, of course, but she was a changed person and she hoped they would see that and not treat her as a young girl with her head filled with silly ideas. She knew the de Vries family had different views on religion and were landed gentry, whereas her parents, though by no means poor, were simple country farmers of the Dutch Catholic faith.

She was in love with Pim – she knew that. What did it matter if their backgrounds were different? Why should religion and status interfere with their love for one another?

These thoughts filled her mind and made the uncomfortable journey home pass more quickly.

She was intrigued by Pim's whispered message. What did he mean? Why did he say that she would see him soon?

At first the question was amusing, then it turned into anger. She hated surprises! They had spent a lot of time together, enough that he could have told her of any plans. And, of course, she knew that he had followed her on some of her rides. But she was sure he had no knowledge of that night.

So, why?

She would soon learn what he meant when she arrived home at her farm.

During her stay with the de Vries, Gionne's character had developed further: she was wary, always courteous, and definitely not an extrovert. When she met new people, she weighed them up and quickly came to recognise those who were genuine.

She was impatient with slow-witted people, she hated fools, and detested braggarts or people full of their own self-importance. She found the de Vries natural people who were kind and never showed off their wealth and position. However, some of their so-called friends or acquaintances were different – some arrogant, most rude or vulgar.

At one social gathering held on the estate, Gionne had gone outside to the stables to check on her horse. One of the guests, an odious, fat aristocrat, who stank to high heaven of both stale wine and body odour, followed her outside and made to lift her skirts. She kicked him hard between his legs and pushed him backwards. He fell onto a hayfork that penetrated his back and fat belly. Gionne stood with her hands on her hips and watched as he writhed with pain, his hands waving in the air imploring her to help him, completely unable to move his bulk off the hayfork. Every time he moved, the fork increased the wound, turning the ground red and sticky with his blood. He started shouting and cursing her, but his vocal cords were weak, and no one heard him. Gionne was mesmerised by the sight of his rapidly waning life and could not move as she watched him slowly die. She left him there covered in straw.

It was not until the following morning that he was discovered by the stable boys.

As one of the guests claimed they saw her talking to him in the yard, she was questioned about her whereabouts that night. Gionne confirmed that she had indeed spoken to him; he was an odious drunk and had tried to take advantage of her but she would elaborate no more.

His death was recorded as misadventure by the Sheriff's recorder. It was surmised that he was drunk and fell backwards onto a hayfork that had been left in the haystack handle first.

Gionne listened with fascination to the various discussions and speculations about his death.

♦♦♦

As her coach bounced along the rough tracks heading towards home, she allowed herself a smile as she reminisced over the excitement she felt on her last night at the de Vries' home.

Gionne arrived home later that afternoon to the open arms of her mother and a smile on her father's usually stern face.

She was glad to be home and in familiar surroundings but would miss the grandeur and opulence of the de Vries' way of life.

Over the next month, Gionne settled back into her old lifestyle, riding Anouk, with Bea running alongside-- to dame school every day. She saw Truus of course and always asked after Pim, who was working in the family business running the estate.

At home, she resumed the daily chores for her mother around the farmhouse as well as working in the fields with her father.

Early one morning, towards the end of her first month home, a visitor rode into the farmyard. Her father came to greet him.

'Greetings Commissioner Hendricks! What brings you out here at this hour?'

'Janus, please! It's Johan. Can we speak somewhere in confidence?'

'Of course! Please come into our home.'

He led the giant of a man into their front room and asked Lenje to leave them. Johan was dressed in his heavily-embroidered army cloak, white breeches and black knee-length riding boots.

Gionne ran upstairs and hid on the landing.

Once seated in front of the fire, and as was the custom, Janus sat waiting for the Commissioner to speak.

'I know you are well-connected with all the farmers in this community and we need some help,' he began. 'There have been a number of mysterious deaths recently. Well, not deaths – murders.'

Janus looked shocked.

'This is terrible, Johan. Who has been murdered and where?'

'They are all drifters or vagrants,' he said, dropping his voice to a near-whisper. 'And it appears that they have been run through with a sword from a mounted rider. Their bodies were hidden or rolled into the dykes.'

'How many are we talking about? Janus asked.

'So far we have found five bodies, all on the roadway to town.'

Janus looked horrified.

'I must warn Gionne to be careful as she rides to school.'

'Do you think you should accompany her?'

'She always takes her dog Bea with her so she will be safe. Besides, she can look after herself.' Janus did not add that he gave Gionne fencing lessons. As if to support his claim, Bea trotted into the front room and collapsed in front of the fire at their feet.

'I see what you mean, Janus – her Keeshond is magnificent.'

Upstairs, Gionne was listening to every word. She smiled; her father had unwittingly placed her as the possible culprit, but it would never occur to the commissioner that a feeble young girl could possibly be the murderer. She decided to bolster these thoughts, so she skipped downstairs.

'Gionne!' her father said, surprised to see her.

She stood still.

'Pater – sorry! I was just upstairs changing.'

'Johan, may I introduce my daughter, Gionne.'

He looked her up and down with a smile on his face.

'I am pleased to meet you. I am Commissioner Hendricks. I'm surprised we have never met.'

'Gionne has been spending some time with the de Vries family and has only been home a short while,' Janus explained.

'A very respectable family. So you ride to school, do you?'

'Yes, on Anouk my horse, and with Bea running alongside.' She kept her reply short.

'Your hound is a magnificent beast,' the Commissioner replied.

'Am I safe riding to school, Pater?' she asked.

Janus looked uncomfortable, aware that Gionne had overheard them talking.

'I am sure you are, Gionne. After all, you have Bea with you and as long as you don't stop, you can't come to any harm.' He touched her face gently as he spoke.

'So, who are these poor people who have been murdered? And where exactly did it happen?' she asked with morbid interest.

The direct questions took Johan Hendricks by surprise.

'Gionne, remember your manners,' her father castigated.

'But it's horrific to think that there is someone out there killing people with a sword,' she said.

Both Janus and the Commissioner stared in shock at her, just as her mother entered the room.

Her father sat down and beckoned Gionne to stand in front of him. She was tall and towered over her seated father.

He took both her hands in his and looked grave.

In that second, Gionne realised what she had said.

Janus stuttered his words: 'H... h ... how did you know they were killed with a sword?'

Gionne shrugged casually.

'I just presumed. A sword, a knife maybe ... couldn't have been a rifle as someone would have heard it. It's the obvious choice,' she bluffed.

Lenje rushed to her side. 'I'm afraid our daughter has a very vivid imagination, sire! She reads too many books that she gets from boys at the academe.'

Or from Pim, she thought to herself.

Johan Hendricks began to laugh.

'Yes, I can see she has Lenje! You have a very bright daughter, Janus. I won't detain you any longer from your work. Just be vigilant and keep your family safe until we catch whoever is killing these poor people.'

With that he swiftly left the room, mounted his horse and waved goodbye. He pressed his mount into a gallop down their lane.

The three of them stood watching the Commissioner and his horse vanish into the mist.

Gionne thought it interesting that no one had pieced all the facts together: she was an expert with an épée, an accomplished rider and a strong girl for her age, but it would not occur to them that *she* could have committed these killings. She smiled inwardly.

'Gionne, come into the house. Your mother and I have something to tell you.'

She was curious.

'We will shortly have a guest staying with us for a month or two. Pieter de Vries, has asked if his son Pim can work on our farm to learn agriculture as part of his education.'

Gionne's eyes lit up. It was all she could do to keep her emotions in check.

Quickly composing herself, she replied in a disappointed tone: 'Oh … him.'

'Why do you say that Gionne?' asked her mother. 'We thought you liked him and Truus. Was he disrespectful to you when you were at their house?'

'No, not at all. I just find him boring, that's all.'

Her mother sensed immediately it wasn't true. Both Truus and Maritje had told Lenje how well Gionne and Pim got on and how they were almost inseparable, much to Truus' annoyance.

'Well, he is coming for a few months, so you will just have to learn to get on with him,' said her father firmly. 'Besides, he will mostly be in the fields with me, so you can spend more time with your mother showing her what skills you have learnt at school.'

Gionne ran up to her room and threw herself onto her bed. She was beside herself with excitement.

♦♦♦

Next day she galloped all the way to school, poor Bea was panting heavily when they arrived.

As she was putting Anouk in the school stable, she saw her best friend arrive in her stately coach.

'Truus!' she called as soon as she saw her friend step out of the coach. 'Papa told me that Pim is coming to stay with us soon.' Glee lit up her face.

Truus was unhappy and showed it: she stiffened, threw her head back and, looking down her nose, said in a cutting voice, 'That's nice for you. I'm sure Pim will be the perfect gentleman. If you will allow him to be.' Truus turned to walk off.

Gionne was taken aback and rushed after her.

'What do you mean? What's wrong Truus? I can ask Papa if you can come as well, as long as you don't mind sharing my bed ... you know... as a kind of chaperone. We can ride together to school.'

Gionne rarely had a cross word for anyone.

'My parents would not allow that and you know it. Throw all your flattery at my brother's feet – I know you have a fondness for him.'

Truus stomped off into school leaving Gionne hurt.

She spent the day in great sadness, wondering what she had done wrong. She thought back over the time she spent with the de Vries and could barely recall a time when the three of them were not together.

She had a special bond with them. At least now her family could reciprocate the de Vries' generosity.

CHAPTER FOUR
Pim

Pim arrived a few weeks later in time for harvest. Lenje had cleared out the spare room next to Gionne's up in the attic and made it cosy with the best bed linen.

Gionne was excited at the thought that he would be here for all that time and with just her for company. She had so many plans to take him on picnics and into the local village.

Over supper each night, they had discussed at length how they expected Gionne to behave and drove the point home that Pim was here to work and learn, not to play or socialise.

'Surely he will need some time off work to rest,' Gionne had protested. 'Then I can take him riding with Anouk and Bea, to show him our lands.'

They both consented that he would need some rest time, so agreed she could take him out, but only once they had both finished their chores.

Pim spent the first week in the fields with Janus learning the layout of the farm, the different crops that were grown and basic arable cultivation for vegetables and flowers. They started before sunrise and came back after sunset, exhausted.

Supper was eaten in relative silence although Gionne was excited to ask him a thousand questions only to be reined in by her mother. The pair saw little of one another.

By the end of the first week, Gionne overheard her father saying that he was impressed with the lad, who was attentive, hardworking and a quick learner – clearly very intelligent.

She beamed with pride, as she had greater designs on developing her relationship with Pim.

On the first Sunday, Janus and Lenje went to church as usual, but Gionne asked to be excused as she wanted to show Pim the wider countryside. Reluctantly, they agreed on this one occasion.

She saddled up Anouk and Viggo – both Gelderlander Friesians and, with the faithful Bea running alongside, they cantered out of the yard into the fields and towards the coast.

They rode for an hour and reached the small fishing village of Kronecker. Gionne had packed a picnic in her saddlebag and suggested they rest up near the beach.

'You are a very accomplished horsewoman,' Pim complimented her as they dismounted.

'I'm full of surprises Pim – you should know that by now!' she teased. 'We spent enough time with Truus at your estate on horseback.'

'Yes, but I never realised how well you handle an épée or a steel blade,' he teased.

She gave him a look as if to warn him.

'I would join the army if girls were allowed, 'she said. 'But instead we have to go to dame school and learn about cooking and housework.'

'If you could do whatever you wanted, what would you do?'

They were sitting on a grassy bank, the horses nearby chewing the cud and Bea flat out after running.

Gionne looked pensive.

'I really want to come to your academe and learn calculus, physics and languages, and to become proficient in combat fighting. Ultimately, I would love to become a physician – I am fascinated by the human body.'

She spoke with such passion, Pim was taken aback: 'That is quite an ambition! It breaks all of our conventions.'

Gionne nodded.

'Women are not allowed in the army, or medicine or politics. I think it's unjust that we are not allowed to be doctors or surgeons.'

'You will,' Pim said, encouragingly. 'It's just a matter of time and, who knows, maybe you will be the first.'

Gionne looked thoughtful.

'Can you teach me to use a flintlock and a knife, like you were taught in the cadets?'

'Of course! And you can borrow my schoolbooks now that I have finished with them.'

She smiled at him then jumped up and took a defensive stance, holding her bare knuckles out like a boxer.

'Come on Pim, show me some fighting manoeuvres like you used to!'

Pim stood, unsure of how much force to exert and taken aback by how tough she was. He went to slap her hands and she threw a solid punch into his gut.

'Come on! Don't be such a sissy!' she goaded.

He went to box with her but she was agile and fast, dodging his thrusts, and landing a left hook on the side of his face.

Shaking his head, he countered her and tried to throw a punch into her skirts, finding it difficult to land a punch in her chest because she was a woman.

'Is that all you have?' she jeered.

Pim bent down and hurled himself at her, lifting her onto his shoulder, her legs kicking out of her skirts and her clenched fists thumping his back. He threw her onto the ground and pinned her down, gazing at the laughter creasing her eyes.

He bent over her and they gently kissed.

She was not expecting this: her first kiss at 16 years of age, but soon her arms encircled his neck, encouraging him to kiss her again.

'You are beautiful, mad and brave, and I have strong feelings for you, Gionne,' Pim whispered.

'Me too,' she said simply.

'You mean, you agree that you are beautiful, brave and mad?' he teased.

'No silly! I mean I have feelings for you as well. Have done ever since my time at your estate. Anyway, you said mad and brave, not brave and mad,' she corrected.

'You are also bright and beautiful, and I too fell for you at home,' he said gently caressing her hair.

Bea decided to join in and started licking them both, standing over Gionne in a protective way.

'Bea! Please let my beau kiss me again,' she asked of her faithful hound.

'Your beau?' he asked. 'Aren't we going too fast here?'

She studied him for a while.

'We need to be very discreet when at home with Mama and Papa. They won't like it if they find out – especially my father.'

'Why? Because you are too young?'

'No, because you are an aristocrat and the wrong religion,' she said.

'What does that matter?' Pim replied. 'I can give you such a different life. And if you want to become a physician then my family can make it happen, I'm sure.'

'Oh Pim. Please don't make it difficult at home! But do teach me unarmed combat … Come on!' Gionne got to her feet again.

To anyone passing, it looked like they were having a genuine fight, as Pim took Gionne through the basic steps of fighting the army way.

Pim soon realised that Gionne was a tough opponent and gave as much as she took. She was unbelievably strong with a very tight grip from years of practising swordsmanship with her father.

'Will Bea be alright with us fighting?' He asked with concern?

'Of course! Bea, lay down and stay,' she commanded.

Each time he taught her a manoeuvre, Gionne copied and gave back twice as hard. He showed her how to hold a knife and how to wield it so that it would inflict serious wounds. He showed her some basic wrestling moves and held her in a tight grip so that he could smell her body and perfume.

She countered the hold and licked his face and neck, blowing in his ear for good measure.

After a while they stopped as Bea was getting agitated at seeing her mistress manhandled by Pim.

They walked their horses slowly back to the farm and arrived in time for supper.

Gionne spent every night in her bedroom studying the books on maths, physics and anatomy that Pim had secretly given her. It was hard going with only a single candle to see by and always a watchful eye out for her parents. Fortunately, their bedroom was on the ground floor so they had little need to come into the attic, where her room was.

Pim answered her many questions as much as he could, and he quickly realised the grasp she had on the subjects having read about them only once.

She never ceased to amaze him.

At dame school, she was constantly asking questions about the subjects she was learning at home and asked why they didn't teach ladies these subjects. Her teachers and the head grew increasingly worried, as Gionne began to stand out from all the other girls.

Truus was most put out by Gionne's seemingly close relationship with her brother and saw the changes in her character. She felt that they were no longer best friends.

At home over supper, Pim and Gionne shared details of their day's outing, leaving out the lessons in combat. But Lenje noticed a change in both their demeanours and that some of their clothing was dishevelled and torn. She didn't say a word.

The weeks passed and Pim found Gionne a formidable swordswoman. They would practise in the yard under the watchful eye of Janus, coaching and teaching both young students. He was secretly proud of his daughter being able to beat this aristocrat's son, particularly at a sport he should excel in.

♦♦♦

Lenje was becoming aware that the relationship between Pim and Gionne was developing into something much stronger by the little signs they both gave, such as the brief brush of hands as they passed each other and the shy smiles they exchanged. Pim would unconsciously stare at Gionne over a meal and then suddenly check himself, glancing at Janus, then Lenje to see if they had noticed.

Then one morning, as Lenje was coming down the stairs she caught their short embrace as Gionne was mounting Anouk to go off to school.

She also found books in Gionne's room on subjects she was not learning at school. Boys' books.

Lenje understood her daughter was very bright and had a thirst for knowledge. It was this way ever since she was a small girl. Both she and the priest had struggled to keep up. But her main concern was her husband, who had fixed views about a woman's place. Although he admired his daughter's skills at riding and fencing, he did not approve of her unquenchable thirst for knowledge. And he blamed the de Vries family for encouraging her.

What would he do if he found out about her affections for Pim? Lenje resorted to speak to Gionne privately about it, even though it was against her principle of supporting her husband's wishes. She loved her daughter and had become very fond of Pim too. She thought they would make the perfect couple in an ideal world. But that would never happen, given their social standing and religious differences. She *had* to speak to her daughter.

The opportunity came when they needed to go to Franeker on household errands. They used their cart and Viggo for the hour's drive to town.

Gionne sat next to her mother and held the reins to drive the cart as it rolled slowly over the rough track.

'Are you becoming fond of Pim?' Lenje started gently.

'Oh, Mama, yes! I think I've fallen in love with him. He is so kind and such a gentleman and we have so much in common.'

'I thought as much.'

'Are you angry with me, Mama?'

'No, not angry at all. Love is a very special emotion and when you meet the right man then you should hold on to him but …' she hesitated.

'I know what you're going to say. I'm still too young, he's in a different social class to us and he's not a Catholic.'

Gionne said this with sadness in her voice and slumped in her seat.

'Your father and I both like Pim very much and he is a good man, but Janus will not approve of your courtship. I don't think he has suspected yet, as he's not mentioned it to me, but I've seen you kissing and those other little gestures of affection. It won't be long until he realises what's going on, and Pim will be sent packing.'

Gionne turned to her mother on the bench seat to plead with her.

'He's been teaching me so much about everything I'm interested in. Please can you speak to Papa and convince him that the de Vries are a good family for me to marry into?'

'Marriage?' Lenje was taken aback. 'Has it gone that far?'

'No, Mama, but it will. I love Pim with all my heart.'

'You're not yet seventeen, Gionne and haven't finished at school yet.'

'But I want to go to university in Amsterdam to study to become a physician. Pim's family have strong connections and will help me get there.'

Lenje was so taken aback by this that she said nothing for a long while.

They'd arrived in Franeker before she spoke. 'We are going to have to speak to your father about this when we return, as well as those books you've been reading in your bedroom at night.'

'Yes, Mama,' was all Gionne could say.

After acquiring the provisions they came for, Lenje returned to the subject of the books.

'Did Pim give you those books to study?'

'Yes, Mama. But I did ask him for them. It's not as if he encouraged me to read them – in fact, he was most concerned that I wanted to – but now he understands my ambitions and only wants to help.'

'We'll see about that,' said Lenje sternly.

'Please don't let Papa send Pim away! He needs to finish farming with us before returning home.

Besides, it won't look good to the de Vries after the hospitality they showed me, will it?' she added hoping it would sway her mother.

♦♦♦

The headmistress of Gionne's dame school was acutely aware of how intelligent, inquisitive and how quick a learner Gionne was. She was always happy, polite and popular with her class friends. She excelled in so many ways including, rumour had it, swordsmanship and other male pursuits, which only enhanced her popularity. But her attitude towards the teachers was condescending. She couldn't understand why she was not allowed to study the sciences, maths and, in particular medicine and anatomy. She frequently told her teachers that she wanted to become a physician and they laughed at her, telling her not to be such a silly girl.

In addition, several of the other pupils' parents had voiced their concerns about the influence Gionne was having on their daughters.

After careful consideration, the headmistress finally decided to write to Janus and Lenje asking for an urgent meeting about their daughter's disruptive behaviour. She was concerned that Gionne was not taking her studies seriously and instead, always reading books that the boys would study at the academe. Her friendship with the de Vries girl was worrying, as was her relationship with Pim de Vries. It was simple: the girl had to stop her wandering, conform to the school rules and join the rest of the girls learning to be ladies or she must go.

But there was one major obstacle: the de Vries were such a powerful and influential family in the area and contributed generously towards the school funds, that she did not want to end up on the wrong side of them. However, she also knew that Gionne's family were staunch Dutch Catholics as opposed to Reformists like the de Vries. If there were to be any backlash, she was counting on this religious difference.

She had to tread very carefully

♦♦♦

Pim continued to work in the fields with Janus, and Gionne soon realised that her mother had not discussed their conversation with her father.

On Pim's day off, they would ride off into the countryside, racing their horses as fast as they could gallop along the roads and through the fields. Gionne always packed a picnic for them to eat and lay on the horse blanket in the sunshine holding hands with Pim. They kissed and hugged each other but he was always a gentleman.

On one of these occasions, Pim was due to go home for a day to see his parents but his reluctance to leave Gionne meant the morning had slipped away.

They were sitting by the river and had eaten their lunch of bread and cheese. Gionne turned to face Pim.

'Tell me your deepest secret,' she said, her eyes full of mischief and burning into his.

He was silent at first, just returning her gaze.

'I am falling in love with you,' he said reaching for her hand.

'I am too, with you,' she replied in a casual way. 'But that's not what I meant.'

She paused.

'I want to know what secret you have that only I should know, and it will become our bond.'

He looked puzzled.

'OK, let me help by telling you mine.'

She sat upright, legs curled under her riding skirts. Her face turned serious.

'Now, you must tell nobody of this.'

Pim nodded, a little worried about what his feisty girlfriend might reveal.

'I want to become a physician. I am fascinated by dead bodies and reading about anatomy.'

He was shocked at first as an image flashed before him: surely the spate of dead bodies found in ditches couldn't be her doing? He dismissed the thought at once. Besides, he found the subject equally fascinating.

'Gionne, what can I *say*? It's something I also have an interest in. Pater wants me to join the family business, but I find that boring.'

'There you see! We are equals.'

She was just a normal girl again.

'But wait – your Mama knows your secret and so does everyone at your school. Truus told me.' Pim was confused – her declaration was not a deep dark secret at all.

Gionne leapt to her feet.

'Fight me then Pim!' She stood legs apart and fists out in front of her. She was such a tomboy, but he loved this part of her as they could wrestle – it was the closest he got to holding her.

Soon her 'secret' was forgotten as they play-fought on the riverbank.

Pim told himself, *just a few more minutes and I'll set off.*

Then he lost himself in Gionne's arms.

Unbeknown to them, a neighbouring farmer passed by and saw them. He was alarmed at first as he thought the young girl was in trouble, but then he recognised both of them and kicked his horse into a gallop, disgusted at their behaviour. He would let his feelings be known to Janus when they next met at market.

CHAPTER FIVE
The Search for a Murderer

In the nearby town of Leeuwarden, Commissioner Johan Hendricks was in deep discussion with his army officers.

'There is a murderer on the loose in my ward, and he needs to be caught. These appalling events cannot continue. Surely, someone must have seen something. I want you all to double your efforts and catch this murderer before I get any more pressure from above.'

'Sir, there have been five killings, and they are all vagrants or beggars. Are they so important that we should spend our time looking for whoever is doing us a favour?' asked one of the more daring officers.

'It matters not if they are vagrants or upstanding citizens; they are human beings, for God's sake!' He was getting agitated.

'Sir, if I may?' asked another officer of more senior rank.

Commissioner Hendricks indicated with his hand for him to proceed.

'If I recall properly, the Sheriff investigated the death of Her Pedersen at the de Vries residence and concluded it was one of misadventure. He apparently fell backwards onto a hay pitchfork in their stable block in a drunken stupor. It occurs to me that the Sheriff did not conduct a thorough investigation – it's not easy to meet one's death in this manner, unless someone was holding the fork for Her Pedersen to fall onto.'

'What are you implying Captain Leijtens?'

'That this too could be murder. They could all be linked. I think the Sheriff's investigation should be reopened to see if there are any similarities.'

Commissioner Hendricks looked thoughtful and responded: 'With the vagrant murders, they were all run through with a steel blade. They were all travelling along a dyke. They were all killed a dusk. And of course, they were all vagrants or beggars. It's likely the assailant was on horseback and practised in the art of swordsmanship. An army officer perhaps or a gentleman.'

'So where is the connection with Her Pedersen?' asked another officer.

Captain Leijtens was quick to answer: 'The assailant could be part of the de Vries household. It's not too far away from where the vagrants were killed.'

He hoped his commander would take him seriously and appoint him to conduct a thorough investigation.

'That's a preposterous statement Captain!' bellowed Commissioner Hendricks, getting red in the face. He slammed his fist down on the table.

'Have you any idea what de Vries would make of our accusations? I would become a laughingstock.'

His face grew even redder. 'No, I won't have it. There is no link at all between Her Pedersen's accidental death and these vagrant murders.'

'But, if I may, Sir …' Captain Leijtens continued.

'No, you may not!' He answered firmly. He stood erect to give weight to his authority.

'I want you all to retrace your steps and question everyone again. Establish their movements on the nights in question, especially anyone who is ex-army, knows how to handle a sword and can ride.'

The officers were dispatched knowing their efforts would be futile; searching Franeker and Leeuwarden for anyone with swordsmanship and riding skills was like looking for a needle in a haystack. They all knew the Commissioner was only worried about his reputation and standing. The murders must stop, and the only way that would happen was by catching whoever was doing the killings.

It was dangerous from both a career point of view, and potential disgrace on one's family, so Leijtens was left in a real quandary. He knew the commissioner was protecting his own position because the de Vries were one of the richest and most powerful families in the country. But he had a gut feeling that there was a link between Her Pedersen's death – no, *murder* – and those of the vagrants. Was he prepared to risk his future, the reputation of his own family and go against military law that states you should always obey orders from a more senior ranking officer?

♦♦♦

Captain Leijtens followed orders along with his officers and soldiers to question everyone in the town and villages, including the surrounding farms. But all the while, he was uncomfortable with it. The only person he could confide in was his 1st Lieutenant, his cousin Carl Leijtens.

One evening, they were dining on their own as they had dispatched the troops to Franeker.

Hans confided in Carl his concerns and private thoughts and his cousin listened intently.

'There's only one way, Hans!' Carl concluded.

'Go on.' Hans was interested to hear his cousin's view. Although three years younger than

Hans, at 28 years of age, Carl was a fast-rising officer and very bright strategist.

'You are quite right that you cannot disobey an order from your direct commander, but what if the order came from higher up?' One side of Carl's mouth lifted into a smile.

'What? I'm sorry but I don't under ...' His words faded away as he suddenly realised what his cousin was suggesting.

'You can't be serious?' Hans said in disbelief.

'Well, he *is* the highest-ranking officer in our army, and he can override any orders given by officers below him.'

'Isn't there a code of ethics or something?' Hans asked.

'I'm not sure there is. If an officer is making a hash of things, he should be reported to the officer above him.'

Hans looked into his cup of wine, silently mulling over what his cousin was suggesting.

'What are you thinking, cousin?' asked Carl.

Hans was silent for a while, then looked up at Carl and poured more wine.

'Commissioner Hendricks is a buffoon. He spends all his time sucking up to the gentry such as the de Vries and not doing his job properly.'

He took a sip of wine before continuing with his train of thought.

'He was at their house party the afternoon that odious, fat, loathsome Pedersen was killed. He probably deserved it. He was drunk and constantly chasing the female servants, I'm reliably told.'

He paused to reflect.

'But Carl, I am certain these murders are being committed by someone who can ride a horse well and is also a skilled swordsman.'

'So ... that points to an officer, an aristocrat or a schooled gentleman,' Carl said.

'The Sheriff only interviewed the kitchen, stable and ground staff after Her Pedersen was found dead. He didn't interview any of the guests or make notes on the method of his death, except for the fact that he apparently fell backwards onto a hayfork. I am told that the hayfork had been left in the hay with the handle pushed into the bail and the forks protruding. Her Pedersen was drunk.'

Carl knew that Hans wasn't finished.

'And why was Her Pedersen in the stable yard? Was he chasing a bit of skirt, a maid perhaps? From memory, it's quite a way from the banquet hall and gallery, where the party was being held, to the stable yard.'

'Unless Her Pedersen was leaving the party and went to find his horse?' Carl ventured.

'No, he arrived by carriage, apparently,' Hans said.

'Why did the Sheriff not conduct a more thorough investigation?'

'Commissioner Hendricks intervened.'

'Ah. And how do *you* know so much already?' asked Carl, leaning forward with interest.

'Oh … I read the brief notes the Sheriff made as I was curious.'

'Does Uncle Albert know the de Vries family?'

'I don't know. I don't recall him ever talking about them, but then I hardly ever saw my father.'

'But you have obviously been to the de Vries estate and hall before?' Carl noted.

'Yes, about two years ago to school young Master Pim in the art of swordsmanship.'

Hans looked up suddenly at his cousin. 'You don't think …?'

Carl grinned. 'It's certainly possible. But it's a double-edged sword – pardon the pun. On the one hand it could all go your way, and you could become our next commissioner, *or* Uncle Albert will dismiss it out of hand and God knows where you will be sent.'

'Thanks Carl! It was your idea in the first place.'

Uncle Albert was Major General Albert Leijtens, commander of the army in the Dutch Provinces. He was powerful and did not suffer fools or incompetence from anyone, including his own family.

Hans resolved to bide his time until the opportunity arose to discuss his theory with his father.

◆◆◆

The search for anyone with the skills of the sword turned up a few of the local gentry, each of whom was outraged at any insinuation that they could be killers. Consequently, the whole community was up in arms with the Commissioner.

Eventually, the outrage felt by the whole community with the way the Commissioner was conducting his investigation caused Major General Leijtens to visit Leeuwarden. He commanded all his officers to attend a briefing including the Sheriff and the Commissioner.

Both Hans and Carl were in attendance but were instructed directly by the Commissioner to keep silent and leave the briefing to him and the Sheriff.

As expected, the meeting very quickly descended into farce as the Commissioner and Sheriff tried to cover up their mistakes.

Major General Leijtens was having none of it.

'Poppycock! Absolute poppycock, Commissioner!' he bellowed. 'I have it on good authority that you have been withholding the truth from me, frightened to upset the de Vries.'

The red-faced Commissioner openly glared at Hans and Carl.

'It's no good glaring at my son and nephew. They are not my source of information and, as enlisted officers, I would expect them to follow army protocol.'

'I'm sorry Major General. I was not implicating Captain Leijtens or First Lieutenant Leijtens. The investigation has been somewhat hampered by the information we have, as the assailant appears to have swordsmanship and riding skills, pointing to the gentry.'

'So has Pieter de Vries been advised of this so we can rule out any of his household and retainers?'

'No, we have not got that far.'

'Well do so immediately or I will take my son and nephew to do the questioning myself.'

Commissioner Hendricks was not a happy man.

That evening Hans and Carl dined with Albert in his quarters.

'That Hendricks is a buffoon and incompetent. I am going to remove him from office as soon as this whole affair has been cleared up.'

Hans hesitated, but Carl gave him a nod.

Sharp as a knife, Albert Leijtens growled, 'Well, come out with it. You have been trying to say something to me all day. It will be kept in confidence, so don't worry about having your head knocked off your shoulders, my boy.'

Hans hesitated as he gathered his thoughts then laid out his whole theory in detail in front of his father, with Carl interjecting on some points.

With his wine glass full, Albert took a deep draught and sat staring at the documentation on the dining table.

'This is very impressive, Hans. You have done me proud.' He looked from Hans to Carl with a raised eyebrow.

'I take it you have presented this to that buffoon Hendricks?'

'Yes, we have, Pater.'

'And I take it he dismissed it straight away as foolish or presumptuous?'

'That's correct. He told us in no uncertain terms not to discuss this with you.'

Albert threw back his head and belly-laughed so loudly he spilt his wine across the table.

'Well, let us put your theory to the test tomorrow. I will personally visit de Vries with you both and let's see if they are harbouring a killer.'

'What about Hendricks?'

'Leave him to me.'

♦♦♦

The world around them was changing and Albert Leijtens knew his command here would change soon.

The American Revolution was causing the English to become exasperated with the Dutch because they were continuing to expand their profitable trade into New America as well as France. Open hostilities were beginning to put a burden on the Anglo-Dutch relationships and the Dutch navy were utterly unprepared to go into battle against the powerful British fleet.

♦♦♦

The next day, a troop of twenty riders trotted unannounced into the courtyard at the de Vries mansion.

Pieter and Maritje were shocked that this Major General would dare force his way into their home without formal invitation.

'It's a matter of murder, Her de Vries,' said Albert Leijtens standing his full five foot two.

'What is it you want and where is Commissioner Hendricks?' asked Pieter.

'Hendricks has been relieved of his command and my son Hans here is the new Commissioner.'

'That decision has to be reached with all the state families – it's not yours to make alone.' Pieter was most indignant.

'I think you will find, Her de Vries, that it is at my sole discretion.'

Albert Leijtens paused for effect.

'Now, to the matter in hand: we believe that the perpetrator is a gentleman skilled in horsemanship and swordsmanship, and we have been interrogating everyone in the towns and villages who meet the criteria. Everyone, that is, except your household and retainers. And so, we wish to discuss this with each of your people, starting with you Her de Vries and your son Pim.'

He looked around the room as more staff started gathering.

'We are including in our enquiries the apparent accident of Her Pederson as the report from the Sheriff is unconvincing.'

Pieter de Vries, though furious at the intrusion, had no option but to gather all his staff and retainers who were in the vicinity.

♦♦♦

Pim, who had been home less than twelve hours, was watching and listening unseen from the balcony that encircled the reception hall. He did not want to be interviewed; his skills on horseback and with a sword or épée matched the criteria. He would not be able to keep this to himself if put under scrutiny. He knew he must escape the house unseen and get back to Gionne.

♦♦♦

It took quite a while to organise the household staff into those that qualified for an interview and those that did not. Messengers were sent out to the tenants and retainers who lived on the estate demanding they attend the Hall immediately.

The senior ranking officers were assigned rooms in the Hall in which to conduct the interviews and had a set of questions for which they needed answers.

Over the course of the day, it became clear there was no evidence of the perpetrator being attached to de Vries household – apart from possibly young Pim, who was nowhere to be found.

They did not consider any females, as they could not imagine any ladies had the ability to ride and wield a sword at the same time.

With each avenue leading to a dead end, Albert Leijtens ordered the immediate apprehension and arrest of Pim de Vries.

CHAPTER SIX
On the Run

Pim had packed a canvas saddlebag with a few clothes and as much money as he could find in the Hall. He snuck through the servants' quarters, into the kitchen and out to the stable yard, where he quickly saddled Viggo.

To avoid being seen, Pim took to the fields to cross their land, and headed onto the north road that would lead him to Gionne's village. Instead of cantering on the narrow track, he stuck to the cropped or fallow fields alongside, which would enable him to hide from any traveller he may encounter, disguising himself as a farmer tending his fields or animals.

It took him the whole day to reach Gionne's village and it was too late to go to her farm.

There was a small village shop and, conscious of being recognised, he pulled his riding cap over his eyes and bought bread, cheese and a jug of beer.

Pim found an abandoned derelict cottage a few kilometres outside of the village. After making sure it was safe and clear of anyone else, he made camp by drawing straw bales into a corner under a part of the roof that seemed relatively solid. He unsaddled Viggo, fed him some hay and led him into the cottage.

He used his saddle as a pillow and wrapped himself in his cape to settle down for the night.

As he stared at the starlit sky through broken and missing tiles, Pim made his plans: they must both escape the country. He was keenly aware what a sacrifice he was making to be with Gionne.

At first light a low mist engulfed the fields, and a slight drizzle dampened the air as Pim saddled his horse. He welcomed the conditions, which would aid his invisibility to others. He was worried about how quickly news would spread that Pim de Vries was on the run from the authorities; in this part of Frisia, his family was not respected.

Gionne's farm was a short canter from here and he fervently hoped her mother and father were working the fields. He wanted to be alone with her to persuade her to leave with him.

♦♦♦

Gionne had arrived home late the previous evening. Anouk was sweaty from a hard ride. The first to greet her was Bea, who barked excitedly so much that her father opened the door in surprise.

Lenje came to the door as well and pushed past Janus, who was dominating the doorway, hands on hips.

'Oh, Gionne, my daughter! You are home!' She gave her a warm hug then immediately pushed her away.

'Why are you so late?'

'And why have you ridden Anouk so hard?'

asked Janus irritably, taking the horse's reins and walking her into the stables.

Gionne shook her mother off and headed straight upstairs to bed.

She heard her parents arguing downstairs before her mother said in no uncertain terms, 'Leave her to me Janus.'

The stairs creaked as Lenje heaved herself up them into the loft space of Gionne's bedroom.

Lenje said nothing, just sat on the edge of the bed and stroked Gionne's hair soothingly.

Eventually she spoke: 'Whatever is going on, I trust you, my daughter. When you think the time is right, come and talk to me.'

After a few minutes and with no response, Lenje stood up and made her way back down the stairs.

Gionne lay there, her mind racing. She stayed in her room all the rest of that night and came down the following morning in her work clothes ready to go to work in the fields before breakfast.

♦♦♦

At the de Vries house, all hell had let loose, as Major General Leijtens ordered a search for Pim de Vries and placed Pieter and Maritje under house arrest until he was found.

They were flabbergasted and ordered a footman to go to their lawyer with an urgent message, sending a second footman to the Dutch Government office in Amsterdam.

Late that afternoon, a general meeting was called in the main ballroom. All the officers in attendance stood behind their respected senior officer, who sat at a long table. Pieter, Maritje and Truus de Vries were at one end with their chief footman, and senior staff members; Albert Leijtens was at the other with his son and nephew.

'I want to know where Master Pim has gone,' he stated forthrightly.

'My son is his own man and not required to tell me his whereabouts, nor what events he has in his social diary,' Pieter replied firmly.

Leijtens banged his fist on the table with such force all the glasses, water jugs and other items leapt into the air.

'Don't you dare lie to me! You may be well connected but I am trying to solve a series of vile murders and your son seems to fit the criteria. We have ruled out everyone else who could be eligible, and your son is the only one without an alibi. We therefore need to talk to him urgently.'

The Major General seemed to have a very short fuse and it was clear that everyone around him was scared to death, including his son and nephew.

Pieter sat holding Maritje's hand and in a very relaxed and aristocratic voice, said, 'I repeat myself Major General: I am not my son's keeper, and might I remind you that you are in my house, on my estate, uninvited. We have given you every courtesy and assistance and I will not tolerate your rude behaviour.'

He paused to let the Major General puff out his cheeks once more then added.

'Now, would you do me the courtesy of leaving my home, and leave my family in peace. If Pim returns, we will inform you. Now go.'

There were rumblings of comments from the estate staff, some of whom resisted the temptation to clap. The officers stood in complete silence not knowing how to react.

Hans and Carl Leijtens both looked at the Major General and stood to leave.

Leijtens sat for a while staring down the table, then stood abruptly and walked out murmuring and coughing under his breath.

◆◆◆

Pim was about to saddle up Viggo, when his horse let out a loud neigh and stamped his front hoof. Pim looked anxiously at his horse and dragged open the broken door to peer out. Nothing. Perhaps Viggo was just picking up on his own nerves.

Pim was still very wary and hesitated before leaving the relative safety of the old cottage.

He would use the misty weather to make his way on foot towards Gionne's farm, leading Viggo quietly behind him

◆◆◆

As they were mounting their horses to move out, Carl saw Truus de Vries walking around the flower garden and remembered her pretty friend from dame school. He racked his brain to remember her name and where he had last seen her.

'Major General, Sir. I have a small errand to run and with your permission, I will catch up with you shortly.'

Albert and Hans looked over at the young lady in the garden and smiled in unison. They spurred their horses into a walk and headed down the long driveway.

Carl dismounted then walked through the walled garden into the flower garden to meet Truus, removing his helmet and folding his white riding gloves into his belt.

'Miss de Vries, I'm glad to have the opportunity to see you before we leave.'

She looked quizzically at him.

'Why would you want the opportunity to see me? Don't you think you and your uncle have done enough damage to our good nature and kindness?'

'I wanted the opportunity to apologise for my uncle's rather gruff military approach to a delicate matter.'

'And my brother?' she asked looking directly at his eyes.

'It's unfortunate that he has done himself no favours by leaving your home without stating where he was going. It places great suspicion on him as he is the only male we have not interviewed.'

He paused. 'We are determined to arrest the man who has murdered these people in cold blood.'

'But I understand they were all vagabonds and beggars,' Truus said.

'Just because they are of low birth or have fallen on hard times, does that not give them a right to fair treatment?' He paused again to read her mind. 'If it were six of your house staff or villagers, would you have a different view?'

'If you put it that way, then yes, I suppose I would.'

He took her elbow and guided her into a slow walk around the flower garden.

'You have a beautiful home here. Your family is one of the oldest in Holland, I understand.'

'I believe so, although it does not matter to me as much as my parents and brother.'

'You attend dame school in Leeuwarden? He asked, changing the subject.

'You are well informed, Lieutenant.'

'Do you travel every day? It must be quite a journey?'

'No, I have rooms in the school I share with others and come home at weekends.'

'And your brother Pim has just finished at the academe. I presume he will go into the family business?'

'Why are you asking these questions?' she said suddenly wary of this handsome officer.

'I'm just making polite conversation. I am interested in your family and how over generations they built such a huge empire. I gather your family are in shipping, farming, and the jewellery trade in Amsterdam.'

Truus nodded.

'I am sure Pim is being groomed to take over from my father eventually.'

'Who was that pretty young friend you had staying here recently? I've not seen her of late.' He tried to ask the question as casually as he could.

'Gionne. She had to return home before the new term starts.'

'Gionne is a roommate then?'

'Yes, and a close friend, too.'

'And where does she live?' he asked.

Truus suddenly became aware that maybe Pim had returned to Gionne's farm and saw through the officer's charm.

'I'm sorry but I am late for my mother. Please excuse me.'

And with that she gathered up her dress, trotted out of the flower garden and through the nearest door into the Hall.

Lieutenant Carl Leijtens was left with just a Christian name – pity, but that would be enough to go on. He smiled at his achievement.

Back at headquarters in the barracks, he asked for a register of those living in the Frisia District.

'What did you want to do, Carl, ask for her hand in marriage?' Hans teased as he brought in the huge register.

'Do you remember that very pretty girl who was constantly with Truus de Vries. The tall one with long auburn hair and a slightly wild look in her eyes.'

'Yes, I do. Rather a tomboy I would say.'

'Her name is Gionne and she is at dame school with Truus in Leeuwarden. I have a gut feeling she will know where Pim de Vries is hiding. Help me with these registers.'

'Would it not be easier to ask the school?'

'That would give the game away. I don't want anyone alerting the girls.'

They spent several hours going through the register until Carl said, 'I think I've found her. She is the only daughter of Janus and Lenje van't Kroenraedt and they farm on the outskirts of Franeker.'

'Good work! Let's go and tell Father. I think we should get the troops together for an early start tomorrow.'

♦♦♦

Pim walked through the fields edging the roadway towards Gionne's farm, holding Viggo's reins.

He was nervous and kept a good look out for anyone coming although it was very early.

It took him an hour to walk the distance and eventually, he saw two silhouettes in the field ahead, bent over hoes. He tied Viggo to a tree in a copse and leapt into the ditch for cover. One of the figures was a large man – Janus; the other was clearly recognisable as Gionne. His heart raced. He was hoping not to meet Janus or Lenje just yet; he wanted time alone with Gionne.

Anouk was strapped to their cart as they loaded the vegetables they were harvesting. She suddenly raised her head and sniffed the air then whinnied as great hooves pawed the ground. Gionne looked up at her horse and then stood to look around, hands on hips, stretching her back as she did.

At first, she didn't see Pim, but then a movement low down caught her eye and she saw him waving.

She shouted something to her father who waved her on.

Gionne walked slowly towards Pim with Bea at her side.

'Pim,' she said in surprise, 'what on earth are you doing back so soon? And why are you hiding?'

'Gionne! All hell has let loose at home, and I am on the run from the army officials.'

She hopped down into the ditch, Bea pacing back and forth above them. They embraced briefly.

'They think that *I* am the person who killed all those vagrants and want to arrest me.'

'But you know you didn't, and they won't have a shred of evidence.'

'They won't care. Our family can't help me either. I've come to ask you to come with me to England to set up a new life there.'

She was silent, clearly astounded by Pim's proposal.

He tried to make it sound less final: 'They will eventually work out who has committed these crimes, Gionne, then perhaps we can come home.'

Still she said nothing, thinking.

'My uncle has ships sailing out of Groningen and Delfzijl, and we can get free passage to Hull on the east coast of England. I have a relative who married into a noble family in Flintshire, south of there, who will take us in. You don't need to pack very much, but bring Anouk as we will need our horses, and Bea of course.'

Gionne was taken aback.

'Pim, I can't leave home. I can't leave my parents. We could be on the run for life!'

'Surely that's better than seeing me arrested, tried and hung?' he said firmly.

She hesitated, looking first to Pim, then to her father far away in the field. Eventually she nodded in agreement. Pim looked relieved.

'I will wait for you here. Come tonight, after your parents have gone to bed. It may be worth covering Anouk's hooves in canvas to deaden any sound.'

He added, 'I love you, Gionne and I promise to protect you.'

♦♦♦

Gionne climbed out of the ditch and walked slowly back to where she'd left her hoe. She continued to pull up the vegetables ready to load onto the cart. Her father presumed she had gone to relieve herself in the ditch.

Her mind was racing with all he had told her.

If we stay and they arrest Pim for murder he will hang for it – I won't be able to live with myself. And what if they think we are both involved? Could we really start a new life in England? Should I leave a note for my parents?

She had never felt such turmoil.

She continued to harvest the vegetables, unaware of the passing hours or of her father's eventual approach with Anouk. He began to load her mound of vegetables onto the cart.

Janus spoke to her and got no answer as she was locked in her own world.

'Gionne … GIONNE … GIONNE! It's time to go and eat. Come on.'

She dug her hoe into the ground and walked beside her father, hoping he would not ask questions. Anouk followed pulling the cart.

'We should have the harvest in by tomorrow,' he said.

◆◆◆

Janus was worried about his daughter. She had been cold and distant since she'd come home the previous day.

Since spending time with the de Vries family and at dame school she had changed. No longer was she his little girl but growing into a woman with a strong character.

He wanted to ask her what was on her mind, but Lenje told him to respect her privacy. He guessed it was to do with a boy – with Pim specifically. Janus might be getting old but he remembered all too clearly what it was like to be young.

Pim was a good Jongen[1] and, with his family background, would be a wealthy and well-respected citizen in time. His religion was a minor obstacle. He secretly agreed with his wife's view that Gionne would make a good wife for Pim and seeing them interact when they worked on the farm was proof of their strong friendship.

He suspected that Gionne and Pim's friendship was deeper that just friends and could not stop

---

[1] Jongen – boy

himself wondering if something had gone wrong. Her late arrival home last night suggested there had been some sort of dispute, and he yearned to ask her. But he had to respect his wife's wishes and resisted any personal questions on the walk home.

Janus had been impressed when Gionne was up and dressed, ready for work at the usual time. Apart from a brief break, she had worked tirelessly.

He knew she was an exceptional Meisja[2] and dame school had shown how bright she was, finishing top in her class across most subjects.

In Frisia, where women were usually brought up in domesticity, Gionne broke those barriers with her desire to become a physician. She was headstrong and very capable.

◆◆◆

---

[2] Meisja – girl

At the barracks in Leeuwarden, Major General Leijtens listened to his son and nephew tell him about their discovery.

'Sire, we understand that Truus de Vries has a good friend who recently stayed with the family: Gionne van't Kroenraedt. She lives on a farm near a village called Franeker in northern Friesland. It appears that Pim de Vries was involved with her romantically and we believe that may be where he has gone.

'May we have your permission to take men to Franeker and arrest Pim de Vries?'

The Major General listened with interest and gave his permission. The mounted troop of twelve soldiers under Captain Hans Leijtens headed out towards the northern district at a trot.

CHAPTER SEVEN
Escape

That evening, Janus and Lenje didn't quiz Gionne but instead talked about the farm and village gossip.

After they had eaten supper, Janus went out to check the livestock in the stable and yard, as was his routine.

'You know, you can tell me anything Gionne if there is anything that's troubling you?' Lenje decided to broach the subject carefully.

Gionne looked at her mother and shrugged.

'Your father and I are worried about you,' Lenje added gently.

'Mama, I don't want to talk about it.'

'I understand. All I will say is that I am here when you do.'

Gionne went to her room. She had to be alone to think about what to do. Her options were stark: stay here and face any consequences. Or start a new life in England with Pim, hoping that in time her parents would forgive her, and any investigations would be dropped.

She packed her canvas travel bag then sat at her little desk to write a letter.

Dearest Mater & Pater,
Please don't be angry and upset; when you read this I will have gone.
The authorities are looking for a man who has committed several murders – they think it's Pim, but he is innocent and only desires to protect me. I have to go with him as we truly love one another.
I will be safe and promise that eventually, I will let you know where I am in the new world.
I love you both and am sorry if I brought shame on our family.
Please try to find it in your hearts to forgive me.
I am also sorry for taking Anouk with me.
With all the love in my heart,
Gionne.

She folded the letter and would leave it on the kitchen table for them to find in the morning.

She waited until the moon was up and the house was silent, before she quietly climbed down the ladder with her canvas bag.

Gionne left the letter on the table where she knew they would see it immediately and signalled to Bea to come.

In the stables, Gionne quickly bound Anouk's hooves in the canvas cloth she had prepared. It occurred to her that it was strange she had done this; her subconscious mind had decided long before her conscious mind that she was leaving with Pim.

As quietly as possible, she led Anouk out of the stables and through the courtyard onto the path leading out of the farm.

Pim was in the ditch waiting for her.

Silently he untied Viggo from the tree, led him onto the pathway, where they mounted their horses and galloped towards the coast, Bea running alongside.

They needed to make as much ground as they could by moonlight; after dawn, the road to Delfzijl would become busy with merchants taking produce to the port. They hoped and prayed that no one would see their silhouettes racing away.

Pim desperately hoped his Uncle Maarten would be at the family home in the port of Delzijl.

♦♦♦

Lenje let out a piercing cry just as Janus came rushing in from the stable yard shouting, 'Someone has stolen Anouk!'

Lenje couldn't speak. She handed Janus the letter, which he read slowly, twice.

'I can't believe this,' he said.

Lenje looked shaken to the core, and he realised he was as well.

They stood inside their farmhouse in a tight embrace, both in tears.

'This is not Gionne. She could not have done this!' Lenje blurted out. 'Not our daughter! She was good, well-mannered, truthful.'

'How could she?' Janus shouted angrily.

They couldn't believe it and looked carefully at her handwriting. For certain it was her neat and precise hand that had written that note.

Janus climbed the ladder to her bedroom. Sure enough her canvas travel bag was gone as were her hairbrush and other personal items.

And Anouk was gone; she'd admitted to taking her.

It was real.

Janus started to think about the consequences.

'Lenje, listen to me: we tell no one about this and if anyone should ask, Gionne is at dame school in Leeuwarden.'

'But who would ask?' Lenje did not understand.

'The authorities will come here sooner or later. They'll soon learn that Pim has been working here recently. We show and tell them nothing. We simply say that Gionne is either at school or at the de Vries Landhuis. As for Pim, we tell them we have no idea as to his whereabouts. We must hide her letter so no one will find it.

♦♦♦

Later that afternoon, as Janus was walking back to the farmhouse for tea, he saw a troop of twelve mounted horseman headed by two officers rushing into their small courtyard.

Some of the horsemen held guard outside the gates and some remained mounted in the yard.

The two officers dismounted and handed the reins of their horses to two unmounted soldiers.

Janus dashed breathless into the yard; he was too old to run.

'What is the meaning of this?' he panted as Lenje came rushing out of the house.

'I am sorry to have startled you. I am Captain Hans Leijtens, and this is First Lieutenant Carl Leijtens.'

They both removed their helmets.

'What is it you want with us?' asked Janus.

'Does Gionne van't Kroenraedt live here?' asked the captain.

'She is our daughter, so yes, when she is not at school in Leeuwarden or at the de Vries' Landhuis,' Janus answered.

'She has not come home then?' Hans Leijtens asked.

'Home? Why are you asking this about our daughter?' Lenje cried out.

Janus took her into his arms to steady her.

'Oh no, no, no, no!' she wailed, tears welling in her eyes. 'What's happened to her … what's happened to our daughter?' she cried. It was a convincing performance.

'Please go into the house, Lenje. Let me deal with this,' Janus said gently. 'I'm sure she is all right and has just pulled one of her pranks.'

Lenje went inside and closed the door, listening by the open window.

'Why exactly are you looking for our daughter?' Janus asked again.

'She is wanted for questioning in an urgent matter along with Pim de Vries, who seems to have disappeared as well.'

'Questioning for what, may I ask?' Janus pushed.

'I am not at liberty to say Meneer van't Kroenraedt. But we need to speak to her urgently.'

'Is she in danger?' Janus asked.

'Again, I am not at liberty to say.'

The first lieutenant prompted his cousin with a loud cough.

'We will need to search your house and buildings,' Hans said officially, signalling to his troops to dismount.

'You will not,' said Janus defiantly.

'We have the powers to arrest you and your wife if you do not allow us to search your property. This is an official search for wanted criminals.'

Janus stepped back in horror and surprise.

'Are you saying that our daughter is a criminal?' Janus said in a disbelieving voice. 'What crime could she possibly commit at her youthful age?'

'Stand aside Meneer van't Kroenraedt,' Hans said officially, taking a stance to hold Janus aside as his troops searched outside and Carl took three men inside the house.

Lenje came running out in tears and ran into Janus's arms.

After what seemed an age, Carl came out shaking his head.

One of the officers spoke to Hans.

'Do you own a horse?' he asked Janus.

'We do, yes, but with the harvest in progress we keep it in the top field to bring the cart back.'

'Is it just the one horse?' Hans asked.

'No. Gionne has her own horse, but she takes it to school in Leeuwarden.'

'And you are certain, her horse was not here last night?'

'Why would you ask?'

Hans raised some cuts of canvas material and binding string in his hand.

'This is used to silence hooves,' he said.

Quick as a flash, Janus responded:

'And we use it to protect our horses' hooves from frost and stones.'

Hans looked annoyed.

The other officers came out of the house and outer buildings, all confirming they had found nothing.

They all remounted their horses, except for Hans, who stood very still looking at Janus and Lenje.

'If your daughter does come home, then it's imperative that she contacts us so we can eliminate her from our enquiries. I will send one of my officers to see you in a few days' time.'

He hesitated.

'I must also warn you of the dangers of harbouring criminals. If either Pim De Vries or your daughter have at any time been here and you've not told us, then there could be repercussions.'

With that he mounted his horse and gave the command to ride out.

Janus and Lenje stood watching them leave, both in shock and disbelief at what the officer in charge had told them. Lenje clutched her heart, next to which she had laid Gionne's letter.

Whatever she had done, Gionne was their daughter and they would protect her. They hoped and prayed that Pim would look after her, wherever they went.

Painful as it was, there was nothing more they could do.

♦♦♦

It was a cold and misty morning as Pim and Gionne rode slowly along the pathway, Bea running alongside. It started to drizzle and so they pulled on their canvas cloaks. At least the rain provided some cover – not many people would venture out in this.

The journey to Delfzijl took almost the entire day because they had to dart for cover every time a person appeared on the horizon. They wanted to avoid all contact and any sightings, so that no one could report having seen them.

They kept to farm tracks as much as possible and at one farmhouse, where the door was left open, they took bread, cheese and ham to eat, making sure they were not spotted.

As they approached the outskirts of Delfzijl, they found an abandoned barn and settled there until dusk to dry off. Pim's Uncle Maarten's house was just on the outskirts of town, and Pim was sure they would be welcomed.

Uncle Maarten had a large Landhuis in grounds with a good stable yard. He had made a good living out of shipping and owned several cargo sailing ships that fed the ports along the coast down to France and Spain, up to Denmark and across to England.

At the age of 55, he had retired from life at sea to run the company, which was part of the de Vries empire, and enjoy life with his wife and children. Both his sons worked in the business and would eventually take over.

Considering he was surprised to hear horses' hooves clop into his yard, followed by a knock on his door, he did not show it when he opened the door to his nephew.

'Well, this *is* a pleasure, Pim!' he said warmly, opening the door wider. 'Please come in.'

'Uncle Maarten! We are sorry to barge in on you unannounced, but we find ourselves in a predicament.'

'Gionne, isn't it?' asked Karen De Vries – Pim's aunt.

'Yes, Madam. We are so sorry to trouble you both.'

'Come in out of the cold. You are both soaking wet and tired. Maybe some food and a hot bath?' she offered.

'Please! You are both welcome at any time,' Uncle Maarten said.

Pim looked grateful.

'Thank you both. We must tell you that we are on the run from the authorities, who have been questioning the family and are now looking for us,' he told them.

Maarten nodded slowly; his face serious.

'You are family, Pim, and we will not give you up to any authority. Now, let's get you out of these wet clothes and some food inside you, and you can tell us all about it.'

'Thank you so much, Uncle Maarten. Are Joost and Casper here?'

'No, they are at sea. Joost has gone to Calais and Casper to Rotterdam.'

Karen took Gionne up to the spare bedroom and filled the tin bath with hot water. She pulled out some of her own clothes.

'These may not fit properly but at least they will do until yours are washed and dried. I will leave you to relax.'

Karen picked up Gionne's clothes and disappeared downstairs.

Karen also found some clothes for Pim as he was the same build as Joost.

A few hours later, they all sat around the kitchen table eating the hot food Karen had prepared.

Pim explained the whole story.

'Why don't you give yourselves up?' Maarten asked. 'You're innocent.'

'They won't believe us, Uncle. That Major General Albert Leijtens wants to arrest us and push forward the charges.'

'Leijtens?' Maartin said angrily. 'That jumped-up piece of cod's roe!'

'You know him?' Pim asked.

'Just a bit. Your father and I were at the same academy, but a year above. He was an arrogant, selfish, jumped-up little idiot then.'

'Father didn't acknowledge him when he raided our home with his troop of soldiers.'

'No, he wouldn't have done. You see Leijtens comes from a different family background to the de Vries. He resents our wealth and standing in the Dutch community.'

'Hence the reason he was so rude to Mamma and Pappa during the investigation,' Pim deduced. 'He is convinced that I am the vagrant killer and will charge me and push a conviction through his paid judges.'

'So, why come here?' asked Uncle Maarten.

'Have you a sailing to England in the next day or so we can catch?' Pim asked.

'Yes, there's one at high tide tomorrow, bound for Hull on the River Humber. Are you taking your horses and Bea, too?'

'That's the plan. I seem to recall we have a relative who married into the Bankes family in Flintshire?'

'We do indeed. Harrietta de Vries is your father's and my sister. She married Lord Henry Bankes – the 5th Marquis of Flintshire. I can write you a letter of introduction.'

'We hope to be able to join their household in some position, perhaps working on their estate,' said Pim.

Maarten leaned back in his chair, a pewter mug of beer in his hand and laughed out loud.

'Leijtens will never find you!'

Karen frowned, less confident.

'Maarten, you must swear all the crew to secrecy when Pim and Gionne go on board. Loose tongues will alert Leijtens to their whereabouts, especially if he is offering a reward,' she said.

Maarten thought a while.

'We could, of course, send him in the wrong direction. We have a boat bound for Lisbon. We can spread the message that they were seen hiding away on board just before it sailed. It's going out on the high tide at the same time.'

'What about Viggo, Anouk and Bea?' asked Gionne. 'How are they going to be hidden on a boat?'

'We have livestock crates and will put both horses and Bea in one crate. Only the ship's master will know.'

Pim and Gionne were able to relax that night, sensing they were in safe hands.

♦♦♦

Johan Hendricks was still harbouring a huge grudge against Albert Leijtens, taking over the investigation.

He was surprised that young Pim had vanished along with that pretty young farmer's daughter.

Still, as ex-Commissioner he had some standing in local society, so intended to act as if he were helping with the investigation.

He put out to all his informants that there was a reward for any information about the two.

Hendricks was at the local inn, about to gorge himself on a leg of mutton, when he was approached by a stranger.

'Commissioner Hendricks?' the man asked.

Hendricks' pride meant he didn't correct the man.

'Yes, what is it? Can't you see I'm at luncheon,' he replied haughtily.

'I am told you are asking for any information about a young boy and girl?'

'Yes, yes! What information do you have?' He looked the stranger up and down. He was not dressed in poor clothes but didn't appear wealthy either. Probably a retainer on the de Vries estate.

'I understand there is a reward. May I ask what it is?' the man asked.

Hendricks looked aloof.

'Once I hear what you have to say, *if* I believe its worthy information, I will decide what the reward is worth.'

'No matter, Commissioner,' the man said cheerfully. 'I will go and see Major General Leijtens instead. I will leave you to enjoy your mutton.'

He bowed and made to leave the inn.

Hendricks dropped the leg of mutton.

'No! Forgive me. You will understand I'm approached by many unscrupulous people only after the reward. Please take a seat and have a draught of beer with me.'

He clicked his fingers at the innkeeper.

The man took a seat at the table and thanked the owner for the beer.

'I am being rude. I am Jacob van de Cloos. I am a trader, selling goods brought in through the ports along this coastline and I'm on my way back from the port of Delfzijl.'

Hendricks nodded. 'How do you know about the two young people we are looking for?'

'I was a guest at the de Vries house, when Major General Leijtens came and threw his weight around. I was unimpressed by his treatment of you.'

Hendricks sat upright. He racked his brain but didn't recognise this man.

'I'm sorry but there were so many guests at their Landhuis, that I cannot recall meeting you,' he said honestly.

'I am not surprised – I was assessing the cargo manifests in de Vries' offices with his team so was not present at the party.'

'What have you got to tell me?' Hendricks hoped fervently that this wasn't another time waster.

'I saw two people on horseback and a large dog on the back roads to Delfzijl last night. They were well hidden under riding capes so I could not see their faces. But looking at how they rode and their slim outlines, I concluded they were not regular travellers. The dog looked like a Keeshond.'

'Where exactly did you see them?'

'I was probably half-a-day's ride out of the port. I was taking shelter from a brief storm when I saw them riding in the direction of the port. They were off the main track and sticking to the edge of the fields, which I thought was strange at the time.'

Hendricks paused and looked at the man. This was vital information if Pim and the girl were trying to leave the country.

'Thank you. The reward for this information is twenty guilders, but we will need to see Leijtens first.'

Hendricks couldn't bear to refer to him by rank. He stood up. 'Wait here and I will fetch him.'

Although Hendricks detested Leijtens – his usurper – he knew an opportunity when he saw one. And information like this was most certainly an opportunity.

Half an hour later, Hendricks entered the inn with the former captain.

After introductions were made, Hans Leijtens recognised Jacob van de Cloos as he had briefly interviewed him.

Jacob retold his tale and asked for his reward – he wanted to make haste to Rotterdam.

'That is very useful, Meneer van de Cloos. We will act on it immediately.'

Hans stood and left to report to his father, nodding his appreciation to Hendricks awkwardly.

Later that afternoon, a troop of twelve mounted soldiers under Hans' command left the barracks headed for Delfzijl at full gallop.

He didn't have time to find out what sailings there were, to where, or who owed the sailing ships. He galloped to the port blind.

They were a good day's ride from Delfzijl.

◆◆◆

Maarten and Karen were up very early and took Gionne and Pim to the *Elija* before dawn so they could board before the docks got busy and no one would see them.

Anouk, Viggo and Bea were put into their crate, hoisted on board then lowered into the cargo hold. There was no one around except for Willem Janssen, the ship's master and a handful of loyal crews, sworn to secrecy. Willem was Karen's brother so totally loyal and dependable.

Whilst Karen was getting Gionne and Pim settled in their tiny cabin for the long voyage, Maarten went to check the manifest for the Lisbon sailing.

He spoke to the master of the Lisbon-bound merchant ship and after a quick explanation, asked him to let the dockside crew know there were two passengers, two horses and a dog on board. He trusted the ship's master, who had been a close friend since school.

On his long walk back to the *Elija*, he bumped into a rotund uncouth gentleman, universally regarded as the town gossip and drunk. Jaap Boerhuis was an extremely nosy, arrogant man who lived and preyed off other people. Maarten took him into the local tavern to buy him a draught of beer, tender a bribe and ask a favour in return.

'I have three sailings today but I can only be in one place at a time. I could use your help, Jaap, to ensure the Lisbon merchant gets underway on time at high tide. Could you keep a lookout? There are two special passengers on that ship and their horses and dog as well. I don't understand why they would want to undertake such a journey, but they paid well.'

'Of course, Maarten! Always happy to help. Do I need to supervise the passengers on board?'

Jaap Boerhuis accepted a small bag of coins from Maarten.

'That's not necessary – they will already be on board in their cabin.'

The Lisbon ship was at the far end of Delfzijl port and therefore out of sight from prying eyes. If any questions were asked, the dockside crew would point the authorities in the direction of the local drunk.

Maarten headed back to the other side of the dock. The previous evening he had written a letter to Harrietta asking her to give Gionne and Pim a place in her household or on her estate. Knowing his sister, she would be like a mother hen to those two, so they would be safe, presuming she could persuade her husband Lord Henry Bankes.

The *Elija* was due to sail in an hour at high tide. Maarten would be relieved once the ship had headed out of the harbour wall.

♦♦♦

It was just turning dusk as a huge commotion erupted in the tiny port of Delfzijl: a troop of twelve sweating, panting horses galloped onto the main dock, their mounts in full uniform, swords drawn and upright in their saddles, reining their horses to a stop, all tired and edgy to a man. The commander shouted orders, demanding to see the harbour master.

'This port is now closed and under my command,' shouted Commissioner Leijtens to the lingering dockside workers.

The harbour master came out of his house, his napkin still around his neck from the supper he'd been enjoying until it was rudely interrupted.

'Sire, how can I be of service to you?' he asked, waddling up to the officer giving the orders.

'We are looking for two young criminals, who are wanted for questioning regarding multiple murders. We are told they came here on horseback; one has a large dog.'

The harbour master scratched his head.

'There was a young couple who boarded the Lisbon sailing at high tide. They had two horses and a dog.'

'What time was that?' Hans asked impatiently.

'Why at high tide, around ten o'clock this morning,' he answered.

'And you are sure they were on board?'

'Personally, I didn't see them, but I know someone who did.'

'Find him immediately!' Hans demanded. 'What other sailings have there been today?'

'There was an England-bound merchant ship that left around the same time, oh – and a few smaller vessels, but they were too small to take passengers.'

'Who owns the ships that left on the high tide?'

'That would be Maarten de Vries, sire,' said the harbour master.

Hans grimaced at the name.

'Well, that's not surprising, is it?' he muttered to himself. 'And where will I find de Vries?'

'At his home or his office, sire.'

'Fetch him and the witness you mentioned to your offices,' Hans commanded.

As the troop dismounted, Hans made for the harbour master's offices, his cousin Carl in tow.

A short while later the door opened, and the harbour master entered with another man.

'This is Jaap Boerhuis, who witnessed the young passengers aboard the Lisbon-bound merchant ship this morning.'

Hans sat in the large chair with one leg arrogantly on the desk.

'Well, what have you to tell me?' he demanded.

Jaap was not sober by this point, having been pulled unwillingly out of the tavern. He stank as he had not washed in months and was a nervous wreck standing in front of this officer.

'It's true a young man and woman went on board the merchant ship with their two horses and a large Keeshond dog earlier this morning.'

'And you witnessed this?'

'Yes, I saw them and I watched the ship leave the harbour walls.'

'You are drunk, meneer and need to take a bath. You stink,' was Hans' reply as he dismissed him from the office.

'Where's de Vries?' he demanded.

'We're finding him, sir,' one of his officers said.

Hans turned to his cousin Carl.

'See what you can pick up around the port, in the tavern and dockside about any sightings. I don't believe that stinking fat drunk. I have serious doubts about his reliability.'

'Yes, cousin.'

There was a light knock at the door, and in walked Maarten de Vries.

'You are looking for me?' he said pleasantly.

'Are you Maarten de Vries?'

'I am.'

'And I take it you own all of the merchant ships in Delfzijl?'

'The de Vries family does – yes,' he answered truthfully.

'How are you related to Pieter de Vries?'

'He is my older brother.'

'And you are aware of the incidents that have taken place in the area of Leeuwarden and Franeker?'

'I am not aware – no sir. What is your business here and why are you asking me these questions?' Maarten was suddenly brazened in his response.

'There have been several vagrant murders, and we suspect that young Pim de Vries is responsible.

We searched Pieter de Vries' Landhuis and grounds, followed Pim's trail to Gionne van't Kroenraedt's farm in Franeker, and on to here, where two people matching their descriptions have been seen boarding one of your merchant ships together with two horses and a large Keeshond.'

Hans paused to get Maarten's reaction, but all he got was a stony face and a shrug of the shoulders. Maarten remained tight-lipped.

'Did you have just two sailings today?'

'Yes. We have six ships altogether and two left today – one for Lisbon in Portugal; one for the Humber in England.'

'And did you have any passengers on either ship?'

'We had passengers bound for Lisbon but not for England, that I'm aware of. Besides, I have not seen my nephew Pim in quite a while.'

He paused for effect. 'But if I may say, I cannot believe Pim is capable of murder. And I know nothing of the lady you mentioned nor his relationship with her.'

Hans sat, staring at Maarten.

'Not sure if I believe you Her de Vries; your family has a knack of lying.'

'That is an outrageous accusation, which I will report back to the family. Now, if you have no further questions, I have ships inbound on the next tide.'

With that Maarten turned and walked out briskly.

Carl reported back shortly afterwards.

'There were two passengers with horses and a dog on the Lisbon sailing, according to several dock workers and, of course, Jaap Boerhuis, the drunkard. Nothing reported from the England sailing that I can find out, cousin.'

'Very well. Is there any way of meeting or intercepting the Lisbon sailing? Does it dock somewhere on the French coast on its journey south? We could have our French counterparts meet the ship. Find out, Carl.'

'Yes sir.' He saluted his cousin.

Hans had a gut feeling that something wasn't right here – that the people were covering up because of the de Vries stronghold on the port. Something told him Gionne and Pim were on the ship to England. He determined to send Carl across to England the next day.

♦♦♦

On board the *Elija* the sailing was smooth for the first few hours after leaving port. Once out of sight of telescopes from the land, both Gionne and Pim came up on deck to stand at the rear of the ship near the wheelhouse. The ship had all its sails up on both masts, as well as the three huge fore sails. The breeze billowed into the canvas sheets propelling the ship across the water at a surprising speed. This was a totally new experience for them. They were both fascinated by the ship's master using a sextant to plot his course and how he knew which direction to go in. The barefoot crew leapt nimbly up the stays to sort out the canvas sheets and hauled on thick ropes to maintain the wind in the sails. They were a happy crew and Gionne could see how they respected the master.

Soon the sky began to cloud over, with dark thunderous-looking clouds in the far distance.

'I would return to your cabin. It's going to get rough in a few hours as we hit the oncoming storm. This is common on this crossing,' the ship's master said. So, they returned below deck to their cabin.

As the ship approached the mid channel, the wind picked up, and the swell increased, hurling angry waves over the bow every time it dipped.

In the tiny cabin aft of the wheelhouse and next to the master's cabin, Gionne started to feel very seasick and asked Pim for a bowl and fresh water. She had never experienced motion sickness before.

She worried about Anouk, Viggo and Bea and asked Pim to enquire after their safety and care in the hold.

As daylight turned to dusk, the crew brought small safety lanterns into their cabin with an evening meal of potatoes and gruel but Gionne had no appetite.

The ship now felt tiny, tossed around as it was on the vicious, tormented sea.

Pim left Gionne to check on the horses and Bea. He held on tightly to ropes, one tied around his waist by a member of the crew. The slippery deck meant making his way to the rope ladder into the hold was tricky. And once he got there, every time the bow plunged into a wave a huge deluge of seawater hit the deck and poured into the hold over him. He wondered how the crew remained safely on deck to steer the vessel through this storm, let alone climb up the rigging to shorten the sails at the top of the masts. It was a miracle in Pim's eyes.

The hold was surprisingly dry, and the animals were safe.

Back in the little cabin, Gionne sat on the edge of a bunk, retching up nothing into the bowl she held tightly in her hands.

Her head was spinning and her body swathed in sweat, even though it was cold. Her shawl hung loosely around her shoulders.

Pim, soaking wet, entered the cabin. He removed his outer coat and boots and his heavy cotton trousers and hung them up on the beam above their head. He changed into his night attire and turned to Gionne.

'I've just checked on the horses and Bea,' he said. 'They are fine.'

Gionne just gazed at him miserably.

'What can I do for you?' he asked in vain.

'Stop this ship from moving!' she shouted angrily.

Pim tried to console her: 'It won't last all night. I spoke to the master, and he said in a few hours we will be through the storm and into calmer waters. This ordeal will soon be over.'

'Let's hope we never have to go back to Frisia,' she said bitterly. 'I don't think I could bear the journey.'

Pim silently agreed but felt sad at the thought he may never see his family again, unless they came to England.

After a few hours the sea became calmer, and the ship resumed its steady course. Gionne's stomach began to settle.

'Let's go up on deck and get some fresh air,' Pim suggested.

Both wrapped themselves up in blankets and climbed the ladders onto the top aft deck, where the helmsman was steering the ship. Willem Janseen had a wide stance, hands on hips as he surveyed his ship.

The clouds had been replaced by a clear moonlit sky and the stars shone brightly overhead like a shoal of tiny diamonds. The moon was large and bright in the northern sky, its reflection brightening the calm sea.

Pim stood behind Gionne by the rails, his arms around her waist as her long red hair billowed across his face in the gentle breeze.

'I do love you, my sweet,' he whispered into Gionne's ear. 'And we will have a good life together in England. I will always protect you.'

She squeezed his strong arms as he held her, and they swayed to the gentle rocking of the ship.

They had no idea what the time was and could not see any land in the distance despite the strong moonlight.

'We should make landfall in a few hours, and by dawn will be near the mouth of the Humber estuary,' Willem offered as he strolled past them.

'Thank you, Master Janseen,' Pim said. 'It was a rough storm but Gionne is now feeling much better.'

'You would do well to have a bite to eat and drink, then return to your bunks to sleep for a few hours,' Janseen suggested.

Willingly, they climbed back down the ladder to below decks again and curled up on the bunk bed in their tiny cabin, falling asleep almost instantly, they were so exhausted.

♦♦♦

In the harbour master's office, reports were coming in about multiple sightings of the youngsters and their animals.

Hans sat brooding, only just keeping his rising temper in check. He was sharp with everyone and clearly annoyed that his quarry had escaped.

As he trusted his cousin implicitly, he sent Carl off to catch a sailing to Hull incognito to try and follow their trail. His brief was to find the pair, follow them and send messages back however he could. Despite what they'd been told, Hans had a good hunch that was where they had gone; the Lisbon sailing had to be a distraction, although it was vital he follow up and confirm that they were *not* on that ship. Six men were dispatched to Ostend to meet the ship as it docked there. He had no confidence that the Belgium, or the Portuguese for that matter, would help them.

He would return to barracks and await news.

CHAPTER EIGHT
England

It was a clear chilly morning when they stood on deck and watched as the ship meandered up the Humber estuary to its destination of Hull. It had to take avoiding action, as the estuary was very busy with small vessels and fishing boats.

Pim wrapped his arms around Gionne's waist and held her tight as they stood in the far top corner of the poop deck, out of the way of the ship's master and his crew.

The land was flat and not too dissimilar to their home of Friesland. They could see many thatched cottages dotted along the coastline, horses and oxen pulling ploughs and carts.

The fishing port of Hull came into sight, and Master Willem Janseen skilfully manoeuvred his ship into the entrance to the busy port to meet the harbour master who would guide him to his dock.

Their first impressions of Hull were of its odour. It stank of rotting fish, cooking, and the urinous faecal pong of human and animal waste.

Once the *Elija* was safely tied up alongside the dock, Janseen helped Gionne and Pim supervise the unloading of the animal crate.

Once Anouk, Viggo and Bea were released, Janseen escorted the couple to an inn that had rooms available. They stabled the horses, fed and watered them, before joining Janseen in the tavern for an ale and some food with Bea begging for her dinner too.

'There's a small ferry that will take you across to Barton in the morning. Claude Smithy is its captain, and he will be expecting you. It departs from the jetty to the right of the port, and I will arrange your passage.'

Janseen had been a terrific help.

'We can't thank you enough, Master Willem, and our family will always be grateful to you,' Pim said.

'That's what families are for. I will let Maarten and Karen know you have both arrived safely here. I hope you find happiness here. Be careful though: I wouldn't put it past Leijtens to have someone follow you over.'

They spent a very comfortable night in their spacious room in the tavern. Spacious at least compared to their tiny cabin on board the *Elija*.

The next morning, they walked their horses, with Bea trotting next to them, to the slipway to meet the ferry and Claude Smithy.

'A message from Willem the Dutchman, said you was coming,' he said.

They paid Smithy, who walked the horses down a gangplank onto the rear of the little vessel and tied their harness reins to the stay. Gionne and Pim sat in the bows with Bea eyeing the crew with suspicion.

Other walking passengers embarked and soon they pushed off. The small sail was hauled up the mast and the bow steered toward the opposite bank on the wide estuary.

The crossing took just over an hour and soon they were safely on the opposite bank of the Humber.

'Need to head in yonder direction, into Flintshire,' said Smithy pointing south. 'And good luck.'

They checked their saddles, tied their canvas bags to the rear of the seats and mounted their horses.

It was going to be a good day's ride to Flintwell Hall.

'Come Bea,' Gionne commanded as they walked out of the town towards their destination.

♦♦♦

A week later, a message arrived at the de Vries Landhuis for Pieter and Maritje from Maarten saying all was well and that Pim and Gionne were safe in England.

They were all relieved and Pieter sent a messenger to Harrietta Bankes – his sister – asking them to extend full family courtesies. He also sent a messenger to Janus and Lenje at their farm.

Truus was in a mood. She was happy that her brother and best friend were safe, but annoyed that Gionne had left her to fend for herself at dame school. She had always found school tricky to navigate and now the vultures and bullies saw Truus had no protection, they started to tease her in and outside of class.

♦♦♦

Unbeknown to the de Vries family, Commissioner Hans Leijtens was intercepting all messages, courtesy of the weak and feeble Johan Hendricks who, despite his fall from grace, would do anything to ingratiate himself with his superiors. It confirmed his suspicions that England was their escape route.

His father Major General Albert Leijtens was not a happy man and was unimpressed by his son and nephew's actions. He blamed their lack of urgency and limited information for their failure. He thought it a lost cause but ordered a watch on the de Vries Landhuis in case the young couple returned.

♦♦♦

A messenger arrived on horseback at the van't Kroenraedt farm just as Janus was returning for supper after a day toiling in the fields.

Lenje came running out of their little cottage, removing her apron at the sound of a visitor arriving at their courtyard.

'Greetings from Pieter de Vries!' the messenger said. 'I have a message for you.' He dismounted from his sweating horse.

Janus took the horse's reins and led it into Anouk's stable for water and feed.

'Thank you meneer, that is so kind,' he said.

'Please come in and have some refreshments. It must have been a long ride,' Lenje said.

They settled him in the main room in front of the roaring fire then gave him some food and a jug of beer.

Janus smiled as he read the letter, before passing it to his wife.

'Good news I hope?' said the messenger mouth full of pie.

'Oh yes – thank you. It's the news we had hoped to receive: our daughter is alive and safe at last.'

The messenger left full and sated on his rested horse for a slower journey back to the de Vries estate.

Just outside Leeuwarden he was stopped by the army troops under Albert Leijtens and interrogated regarding the contents of the message.

'It was a sealed message, and I was not privy to its contents,' he told them.

'Was the message read out loud at any time?'

'No, meneer, they read it and smiled, saying that their daughter was alive and safe.'

After a while and with no more information forthcoming, they released him. He reported to Pieter on arrival at the estate what had happened. De Vries listened with interest. Now Pieter knew

Leijtens was intercepting his messages, he would use this to his advantage.

He sent a new message using the usual channels to Henry Bankes, advising that they had secured a position for both Pim and Gionne in the household of a cousin in Scotland. They would be expected there in three months' time.

He trusted his sister would read into this message; they had no relatives in Scotland.

◆◆◆

Carl Leijtens arrived in Hull a day after Gionne and Pim. After enquiries around the dock in his broken English, he established that the young couple had crossed to the south bank on the morning tide. He would follow, though he had no idea where he was going.

He spent all day in the taverns and dockside food houses, bribing people for information. The English were tight lipped, until one drunk revealed he'd heard something about Flintwell Hall in Flintshire.

That's where he would go. He needed to acquire a horse for tomorrow, but more pressingly, a bed for the night.

Carl needed a plan to get an audience with the Earl of Flintshire and persuade him that Pim de Vries was a wanted criminal in Holland. He knew it would be a challenge, not only with the language barrier – his English was passable – but he had never met aristocratic English people before. Were they very different from the Dutch aristocracy? How would he be received in his uniform?

He was up early and caught the dawn ferry to Immingham. The weather was foul. High winds tossed the little ferry around like a cork in the rough waters of the estuary. Although not raining, the sky was black and ominous. The ferryman didn't seem concerned at all however and was happy to put to sea with a half sail on the mast.

On arrival at Immingham, Carl found he had made a mistake: this was a small fishing port that stank of rotting fish. There were no stable yards anywhere and only one tavern.

He found a drunk who sold him a mule for the price of a flagon of beer.

The mule would get him along the coast to Barton, where he should have gone in the first place, and where he hoped to exchange the mule for a horse.

It took him half a day in the pouring rain on the bad-tempered, wheezing mule to get to Barton, where he eventually found a stable with proper horses.

He learned from the stable owner that there had been a couple of foreign youngsters on two very fine horses, the likes of which he had never seen before. The couple were accompanied by a huge hairy dog.

Having confirmed he was on the right track; Carl purchased a good solid horse – old but ex-cavalry – and left the mule with the stable owner.

Because of the delay and the slow ride from Immingham, night was closing in. Knowing from the locals that Flintwell Hall was a good day's ride, Carl took a room in the local tavern for the night.

Dawn broke with the same dark skies, a ferocious wind and the addition of piercing horizontal rain. But Carl was a trained mounted soldier and this was nothing to him. He just had to wrap his coat tightly round him, pull his hood over his head and grin and bear it.

He knew that he could not present himself to Lord Bankes looking like a vagrant however, so he hoped there would be a tavern in the local village where he could have a hot bath and dry out.

He headed south along the beaten earth, trotting along as fast as the beast would take him. He saw no one on the road, no one in the fields and no one from whom to ask directions. Most of the villages he went through showed little or no life, as if all were closed and boarded up against the foul weather. He resisted the temptation to knock on doors to ask for food, water or directions, unsure what kind of reception he would be given. How would the locals react to a Dutchman in these parts?

Eventually, he came to a larger town and discovered that it wasn't far to Flintwell Hall, and that it had a Mayor and a High Sheriff. The inn he found was pleasant and of a higher standard than those he had frequented since landing in England.

◆◆◆

Following directions from the innkeeper, Gionne and Pim arrived at an impressive wrought-iron gate, which opened to a tree-lined lane of red earth. The lane meandered until finally opening out into a large open courtyard in front of a grand building.

Flintwell Hall was an imposing castle with turrets, clearly built centuries before. It had been the seat of the Earls of Flintshire for five generations of Henry Bankes' family.

A stable hand ran out to greet them, followed by several servants all smartly dressed.

'Welcome Master Pim and Miss Gionne.' The head butler James Howell greeted them warmly. 'Her Ladyship awaits you in the morning room.'

They were both surprised that Harrietta Bankes knew of their impending arrival.

They climbed the stone stairs to two enormous oak doors that opened into a huge high-ceilinged hall. Twin wide marble staircases swept down from the first floor.

Pim and Gionne followed the head butler up these stairs and into a carpeted reception room lined with antique paintings. Long drapes half covered the floor-to-ceiling windows.

Standing by a suite of seats was a tall, elegant lady dressed in very fine clothes.

'My dear nephew, Pim!' she exclaimed in Dutch. 'And you must be Gionne.'

'Aunt Harrietta! We didn't realise you knew we were coming,' Pim answered in English.'

'I only received word from Maarten this morning. Then a second message from Pieter arrived just an hour ago. Come and sit.' She gestured to some very fine couches.

'My husband Henry is away in London on business and returns this evening.'

She turned to the butler.

'Please bring us some tea and a tray of food. These poor souls look hungry and thirsty.'

Howell bowed and disappeared through another door.

'I don't understand how messages could have arrived before us. It was a horrendous journey,' Pim stated.

'Well, they did, and we must get you settled in. Of course, you are most welcome to stay here with us. Mrs Cribb, our head housekeeper, will arrange your rooms in the north wing.'

Gionne took off her headscarf, allowing her long red hair to fall over her shoulders and down her back. She sat upright as she'd been taught at dame school, her long legs held firmly together.

Harrietta turned to Gionne. 'You are a very beautiful young lady, and with breeding, I see. We are so happy that our Pim has found someone to challenge him,' she teased.

'Now Pim, tell me all about your recent escapades and why you have half the Dutch army after you.'

Pim and Gionne spent the next hour outlining everything that had happened.

'So ... if what you say is right, they are blaming *you* Pim for the murders, but have ruled out this beauty, who is strong and fit and – I would wager – handy at any male event, such as riding, swordsmanship and the like.'

Gionne blushed and Lady Harrietta noticed the scarlet colouring on her neck.

'Pim, your father sent me a very cryptic note, suggesting we send you to our family in Scotland.'

'But we don't have any family in Scotland,' answered Pim, confused.

'Quite!,' she replied, smiling.

After a while she sent them with Mrs Cribb to their new quarters with instructions to change for dinner at eight sharp.

Mrs Cribb was a short, rotund, cheerful, elderly lady, who seemed to be very much part and parcel of the family.

'Now don't you go fretting about an evening gown, my lady, as we have found a few that we hope you will like. And you, Master Pim need to smarten up as well.'

In the north wing of the castle on the second floor was a suite of two bedchambers with roaring fires keeping the rooms warm. Each led into a large comfortable sitting room with a huge cast-iron grate, where logs glowed in the open fireplace. A copper slipper bath was set up in the bedchamber designated for Gionne, with dresses laid out on her bed ready for her to try on.

Gionne skipped into Pim's room and threw herself at him. They both landed on his bed laughing with her on top.

'This is so good!' she said. 'And your aunt is wonderful. I can see a family resemblance.'

They kissed passionately for the first time in what seemed an age, feeling safe at last.

Pim was happy for the first time since leaving his family home. It felt good here and he started to relax.

'Come and look at this.' Pim took her hand and pulled her off the bed.

'Have you seen one of these before?' he said, peering into a small round room built into the curve of the turret. It had a rug covering the doorway and a wooden seat was positioned over an open hole that dropped down to a pit of some sort.

'It looks like a privy or what they call a *garderobe*. It's still in use and has been here since the castle was built.'

Gionne grimaced at the sight of it, and blushed.

'I will continue to use the chamber pot, thank you,' she laughed.

They relaxed in their new home and took their time dressing for dinner. There was a gentle tap on the door and Pim opened it to a footman.

'George Bedlan, sire. Her Ladyship and His Lordship await your company if you would follow me,' he said politely.

They were taken to another huge dining room with quite a few finely-dressed people already seated around a long table.

Lord Henry Bankes stood and came to greet them, followed by Harrietta.

'Henry, may I introduce my nephew, Pim de Vries and Miss Gionne van't Kroenraedt.'

Henry shook Pim's hand.

'I've heard a lot about you and your escapades, young Pim. You and Gionne are most welcome into our family, where you will be protected and safe.'

'Come and join our friends.' Harrietta took Gionne's hand and led her to the seat next to hers with Pim opposite, next to Lord Bankes.

'Ladies and Gentlemen, may we present from Holland, my nephew and his delightful wife: Pim de Vries and Gionne. They do speak a little English, but I am happy to translate anything you don't understand.'

She announced them as if they were a married couple, which Gionne found very strange but liked the idea. She glanced over to Pim who was looking at her with a cheeky smile. He gave her a wink.

The evening went so quickly. The six-course meal was delicious but too much and it took all of Gionne's concentration to understand what the aristocratic English were saying. Occasionally, Harrietta would interject and help out, whispering in Gionne's ear in Dutch who the person was with a quip.

'That overdressed lady with too much face cream and an overburdened wig is Lady Penelopy Grace, whose husband owns land up north. They see our home as a stopping point halfway to London. She smells,' Harrietta added and they both burst out laughing, knowing no one except Pim understood what she'd said.

A little later Harrietta whispered, 'This is such fun, talking to you in Dutch and no one knowing what we are saying.'

'Are all the people here nobility?' Gionne asked.

'Most are landed gentry with some titles. Some are hereditary and come from a long line of aristocrats, like Henry; others like to pretend they are important, like the pompous lady you were talking to.'

'That is so amusing.' Gionne was in awe of the gathering.

'Now, I must introduce you to my very best friend, Louise Failsworth – Lady Corringham. Sir Bernard – her husband – and Henry are also old school friends, and we see a lot of each other.'

'Why is she called Lady Corringham when her name is Louise Failsworth?'

'Because Bernard inherited his family seat in Corringham and has the title Lord Corringham, even though his real name is Sir Bernard Failsworth,' Harrietta tried to explain.

'And you are the Marchioness of Flintshire, yet people address you as Lady Harrietta Bankes.' Gionne was confused and fascinated in equal measure.

'Again, Henry inherited the title of the 5th Marquis of Flintshire after his father, also named Henry, died. In fact, every first-born male in the Bankes line has been called Henry since the 1650s.'

Gionne nodded, still confused.

'Don't worry, you will soon understand. Now let's catch Louise before they leave.'

The meal was over, and all the men stood and followed Henry Bankes into another room. The ladies continued to sit in their seats or stood to talk to others. There must have been twenty people in the grand dining hall.

Harrietta took Gionne's hand and walked quickly around to the other side of the huge table to catch Louise.

'Lou, may I introduce my new ward, Gionne van't Kroenraedt, from near my hometown in Frisia.'

Louise Failsworth was beautiful, tall, slim and elegant, with piercing blue eyes and long, blonde hair. Her dress was made of pure silk and shimmered as she moved. She was modest with her cleavage, showing just enough, unlike some of the other ladies who were so shameless it was a credit to the dressmaker that their bosoms were held in place. Others, like Harrietta wore dresses that covered their body from the neck all the way to their feet, as was Gionne's borrowed gown.

Gionne curtsied clumsily.

'No need for that, dear child,' Louise said in a soft kindly voice. 'You are family and it's a delight to meet you. I hope that over the next few days we can become very close friends.'

'That would be wonderful – yes please,' stammered Gionne.

Louise smiled and turned to Harrietta, still holding Gionne's hand.

'She is so beautiful with her long red hair and bone structure. Such strong hands, too. I bet you are more of a tomboy than a refined lady,' she teased.

'Gionne is a very accomplished horsewoman and, from what I understand, is more at home with an épée than sewing needles. I hear from my brother

Pieter that she shunned dame school for the boy's academe and is excellent at maths, physics and anatomy,' Harrietta announced proudly.

'So, a real match for young Pim then?' stated Louise. 'We are going to have such fun with you, my girl, as you compete with our husbands and sons on their level.'

'What do you mean?' Gionne asked.

'We have a games day on Saturday, where we open our house to all to compete in horseracing, duelling, polo and other games,' Harrietta explained. 'Don't worry – we can get you prepared over the next few days. It will be fun.'

Pim and Gionne met at midnight on the grand staircase leading to the first floor. He was drunk, and she was bewildered with all she had learnt from Harrietta, Louise and the other ladies.

They fell into the same bed and fast asleep without undressing. They woke early the next morning, when they undressed one another slowly.

'Did you hear Harrietta announce us as the de Vries, as if we were married.' Gionne said rolling into Pim's naked body.

'That's not a bad idea,' he said, stroking her long red hair down her back as she mounted him.

'Are you asking me to marry you, Pim de Vries?' she said with shortened breath as he penetrated her.

'Well, what's your answer Gionne van't Kroenraedt?' He held her hips to feel himself more inside her.

'God, yes,' she said.

'Is that yes, I will marry you, handsome Pim?' he jested. 'Or are you remarking on my lovemaking?'

'Oh, do shut up Pim! Yes, I'll marry you, now concentrate on me.'

She gasped as he cupped one small hard breast with one hand and gripped her beautiful round backside with the other. Minutes later, Gionne climaxed with a loud cry.

Lying on the bed afterwards, Pim rolled onto his side, arm under his head and spoke.

'Well, I need your father's permission first and how do we get that? Aunt Harrietta will act as my family on behalf of my parents. Should we speak to Uncle Henry and Aunt Harrietta today about when we can marry?'

'I think the right thing to do is to send a message to my parents asking for their blessing and hope that they agree. But you know we are Catholics, and your family are Protestant, and that is not approved?' Gionne was worried.

'It's different here. They don't have the religious traditions we do in Holland.'

'What if my father forbids it?'

'It will be too late by the time we receive an answer back,' Pim said, half joking.

Gionne pushed him onto his back and mounted him again.

'You are insatiable, my Gionne,' he grinned.

♦♦♦

'That's wonderful news!' gushed Harrietta. 'You must have your wedding here, isn't that right Henry?' she asked looking at her husband.

'Without doubt,' he agreed, smiling.

Pim and Gionne exchanged a happy look.

'I want to send this by messenger to Gionne's parents asking permission to marry their daughter.' Pim handed a folded message to his aunt.

'We will get that off straight away, but it will be some time before we get a response,' Henry said.

Pim looked anxious.

'What is it?' Harrietta asked.

'Meneer van't Kroenraedt may refuse,' he said.

'And why would he?' asked Harrietta.

'The problem is one of religion. Gionne and her parents are Catholic, whereas, Aunt, we are Protestant.'

'But you are here in England – an Anglican country, thanks to our dear Henry VIII – and our views on mixed marriage are very different from those in your homeland,' Henry assured them.

'But England split from Rome and created the Protestant religion. Are Catholics now accepted here?' asked Gionne.

'In the main we are Anglican, which opens its doors to both main religions. If there is any single belief that predominates, it's the Christian belief. We now have Methodists and Baptists, though mainly in the west. So, as the Marquis of Flintshire, I am happy to marry you both here at Flintwell Hall, officially,' Henry stated.

Both Gionne and Pim were comforted by Henry's assurances and offer, but Pim was still apprehensive about the response from Gionne's strict parents.

They spent the rest of the evening talking about dates, planning the service in the estate chapel and wondering what message would come back from Gionne's parents.

♦♦♦

Carl Leijtens followed the road towards Flintwell Hall. Intelligence he had collected from travellers and village folk along the way confirmed that a young man and woman on horseback had been through a day before.

He was getting close.

Arriving at the magnificent wrought-iron gate leading to Flintwell Hall, Carl decided to find a secure, well-hidden place in the surrounding woodland on the edge of the estate grounds to set up an observation hide. He had his small telescope and enough provisions to mount a few days' observation. He'd also secured a room at the local tavern in Flintwell, where he would rest and eat.

Conscious that a Dutch foreigner would stand out, he left very early to go to his post near the hall and arrived back after dark. After a wash and change of clothes, he would sit at a corner table to eat and listen to the local gossip. He was desperate to keep a low profile as did not want to arouse suspicions.

On the second day, huddled in his makeshift hide, Carl saw Gionne and Pim walking hand in hand in the gardens. They looked happy and relaxed. Later, he saw them leave the stable yard on their horses with a massive Keeshond dog running close to her mistress's horse as they cantered then galloped around the parkland surrounding the vast hall.

He watched them practise sword fighting with épées in the gardens and they seemed equally matched. She was good.

As he observed them, it occurred to him that they thought they were safe here; they looked at ease – just a happy couple of kids. Though one of them was highly dangerous and liked to murder innocent vagrants, he reminded himself. Their guard would be down and the last thing they would expect would be First Lieutenant Carl Leijtens of the Frisia Army on their doorstep – an advantage he intended to use.

He had to devise a plan to arrest them and take them back to Holland for his uncle.

Could he do this on his own? Or should he try and enlist the help of the locals? He dismissed the notion immediately; they were likely appointed by the Marquis and therefore would be loyal to him.

Maybe he could get word to Uncle Albert or Hans to send troops over? Maybe not. This would involve political and lawful negotiations that would take time. His only option, he concluded, was to try and arrest them himself and then ask for cooperation from the local Sheriff to escort them to the ship at Hull.

On the third night of his stay at the inn, he ordered his usual bowl of stew and bread with a flagon of their warm beer. He sat solitary in the farthest corner of the inn but his presence was soon noticed.

'Who's that?' Randulph Blake, the Flintwell Hall estate steward, asked the tavern owner? Randulph lived with his wife in the village rather than on the estate. He was with Tobias Lilley, one of the gamekeepers and Randulph's wife's cousin.

'Don't know. Foreigner. Has a funny accent. Arrived two days ago and pays for his board and lodging with coin,' he replied.

Tobias chipped in: 'Seen him hiding in the woods above the Hall. Methinks he's spying on his Lordship or the new arrivals.'

Randulph took a draw on his flagon, wiped his beard and walked over to Carl, where he extended his hand in a show of friendship.

Carl looked suspiciously at the hand. It was huge; the man was clearly a land worker.

'Randulph Blake, estate steward at Flintwell Hall.' His hand remained extended.

Tobias and the other patrons at the inn watched with interest.

'Carl Leijtens from Leeuwarden in Holland.' He took Randolph's hand and shook it.

'I work for Lord Henry Bankes, the Marquis. Are you looking for an introduction?' he asked.

'I am interested in a couple of his guests, yes,' Carl answered vaguely.

'Lady Harrietta Bankes is originally from Friesland in Holland, I understand,' Randulph volunteered, trying to open up the conversation. This was news to Carl.

'Come and have a beer with us,' Randulph offered.

Carl was hesitant, suspicious of this giant of a man and his shorter sidekick at the bar.

Sensing this, Randulph signalled to Tobias to bring some flagons over and sat on the stool opposite Carl.

'This is Tobias, one of my gamekeepers.' Carl acknowledged him with a nod.

'What's your business here? You're a long way from home?' Randulph asked directly.

'I have business with Pim de Vries and his female friend,' he answered curtly.

'You will need to ask permission from his Lordship to speak to them, which I am happy to arrange,' he volunteered.

'Are you in the military?' asked Tobias.

Carl looked at him with cold eyes.

'Why do you ask?' he said in his curt accented English.

'Your manner. And your hide in the woods looks like it's been made by a military man.' Tobias looked him straight in the eye.

Carl was startled to hear his hide had been discovered. How long had they known?

He was on edge now. His sword and dagger were upstairs in his room, and he didn't fancy fighting this giant of a man or his friend.

He decided to reveal who he was and ask to see Lady Bankes. If she were originally from Holland, she would understand him better in their native language.

'I'm First Lieutenant Carl Leijtens from the Friesland divisional army. I am here to speak to Meneer Pim de Vries about incidents that occurred in his hometown of Leeuwarden. I also want the speak to Gionne van't Kroenraedt.'

Randulph nodded giving nothing away.

'You do know that Lady Harrietta was a de Vries and is Pim's aunt? I am also reliably informed that the young lady and gentlemen are engaged to be married soon.' He was interested to see the officer's reaction to this news.

Carl was surprised on both counts but his military training taught him to keep a straight face.

'I would be grateful for a meeting with Lady Harrietta if that could be arranged,' he said calmly.

'I will ask her Ladyship in the morning. In the meantime, I would strongly suggest you stay here and don't venture out.' Randulph stood with his flagon of ale, raised it in toast to the young officer and returned to the bar, with Tobias following.

It was late, but Randulph was troubled by his encounter with the stranger. He told Tobias to fetch his horse and they both rode the few miles to the Hall.

Fortunately, Harrietta was still up and saw them galloping up the lane to the hall.

She greeted them herself at the huge oak front door.

'What's the late-night haste about?' she asked.

'Your Ladyship, I have troubling news.' Randulph bowed as he usually did in front of her ladyship.

'Well come in and tell all. Lord Bankes is already in his chambers.'

Tobias stayed outside with the horses and Randulph accompanied Lady Bankes into the small evening room, where she poured him a large glass of porter.

'Now, please sit and tell me what's troubling you.' She sat elegantly on the edge of the two-seater opposite Randulph.

He told her everything that had happened in the tavern and gave a brief description of Carl.

She sat in silence thinking.

'I do remember the Leijtens family. Major General Albert was always a bully at the academe with my brothers. I recall he had two sons but don't remember this Carl fellow.'

She pressed on: 'Did he say *why* he wanted to speak to Pim?'

'Only that it was about a series of events that took place in Leeuwarden.'

She knew immediately he had come for Pim and Gionne and composed herself before giving instructions.

'I want you to ask General Stanley to come and see me tomorrow. You will have to wake him from his drunken stupor, no doubt. And Randulph, tell no one about this.'

'You want me to go and see the High Sheriff tonight, maam?' he asked in amazement, knowing that he would have a rough reception from the town bully.

'Yes, I do, and make sure he is here before noon. Then I want you to ask this Carl Leijtens to come for luncheon just after noon.'

'Yes, your Ladyship.' Randulph stood, bowed and left.

Pim and Gionne had heard his arrival and were listening on the grand staircase. When the coast was clear, they went into the evening room.

'What does Carl Leijtens want, Aunt? Pim asked as they both sat in front of her.

'Both of you, I think. But I have a plan – if that drunkard, General Stanley plays ball.'

'What plan?' Gionne asked.

Lady Harrietta smiled enigmatically.

'Carl is a military man. He is here as a civilian, and my plan is to have him arrested by the High Sheriff on grounds of espionage. Let's see what Albert makes of that!' she said indignantly.

'Albert, Aunt?' Pim asked.

'That bully accosted me when we were young, and I've never forgotten. He has always been jealous of me and Pieter and likes to throw his weight around, especially now he's a Major General.' It seemed Lady Harrietta was about to take her revenge.

Gionne sat silently taking it all in. She thought about the many things she could do: was he a good swordsman? She would challenge him to a duel and beat him. These thoughts consumed her.

Pim was troubled by Gionne's silence.

Lady Harrietta's tone softened as she turned to her charges.

'I don't want you here tomorrow, so I suggest you go and see Bernard and Louise Failsworth at Failsworth Hall. There is always an open invitation to see them.'

Pim and Gionne knew it was more of a command than a suggestion. They walked slowly back to their rooms in silence.

♦♦♦

General Clifford Stanley rode up to Flintwell Hall, as sober as a High Sheriff could be yet still he reeked of stale beer. For a man in his position, he was a disgrace. His clothes were old, dirty and torn. He looked dishevelled and hadn't had a haircut in years, so lank greasy curls touched his shoulders. He was in his mid-fifties and had served in the army in several skirmishes but never gained much of a reputation. He only landed the role of High Sheriff because of his army rank and the fact that he lived in Flintwell village.

In spite of all these shortcomings, he did his job competently and remained sober during the day, dealing with discipline and disputes with surprisingly intelligent reasoning. He was popular with the locals but also known to like a drink.

On arrival at the hall, he was ushered into the morning room where Lady Harrietta sat. He took off his large hat and bowed so low that his greasy hair flapped over his face.

Harrietta had to stifle a giggle and compose herself.

'Your Ladyship. How can I be of service to you?' he asked.

'Please take a seat, General.' She pointed at a sturdy chair brought in to accommodate his bulky weight.

'It's a delicate issue; one that requires your guile and authority as the law in this part of England.'

Stanley felt a jab of surprise and pride on hearing these words.

'It would be my honour, your Ladyship.'

'In a short while we will meet a Dutchman – a lieutenant in the Dutch army from Leeuwarden barracks. His name is Carl Leijtens. He has come to arrest my nephew and his fiancée on jumped up charges made by my nemesis, Albert Leijtens, his uncle. I won't go into detail – it's not necessary for you to know – but this Carl Leijtens is here under false pretences, has been spying on my family, and is potentially here to harm us. So … I want you to arrest him on grounds of espionage.'

Clifford Stanley gazed at the fine carpet under his feet taking in what Lady Harrietta had said. He was trying to decide if it was in his domain to take such action.

'Maam, to arrest him on grounds of espionage, we need to have proof.'

'Yes, we do and that's why he is joining us shortly.'

'He's coming here, today?' Stanley was astounded.

'Yes, in fact, I think that's him coming now.' She pointed out of the window at a soldier smartly dressed in Dutch uniform.

Harrietta smiled as she was hoping he would dress formally; it would play into her hands.

'Just follow my lead, General, and I will lead him into a trap.'

'Your Ladyship.' Stanley nodded and remained seated, still confused.

James Howell, the Head Butler, opened the French doors to the morning room and announced, 'Lieutenant Leijtens, your Ladyship.' He bowed and stood aside for the handsome lieutenant to enter.

'Het is een genoegen u te ontmoeten, uwe Ladyship.' He greeted her in Dutch.

'Please take a seat Lieutenant,' she said in English. 'I understand your English is quite proficient. May I present General Stanley, who is our High Sheriff and also a guest today.' She spoke in a commanding voice.

He shook hands with the General and looked confused.

'I apologise, but I understood we would meet privately. What I have to say is confidential and delicate.'

'Meneer Leijtens, the General is the law in these parts and therefore my guide in anything concerning the subjects you wish to discuss.'

She deliberately insulted him by calling him *meneer* instead of using his rank, which seemed to throw him.

'Kunnen we alsjeblieft prive praten?' he asked in Dutch.

'Anything you wish to say *in private* can be said with the General here,' she said in English.

He was clearly knocked off kilter.

'Very well, your Ladyship.'

'Well, what is it you have to say about my nephew?'

Carl was thrown but had no choice but to continue.

'There have been a series of murders, all vagrants, in and around Leeuwarden over the last three years, which we have been trying to solve. Each was killed in the same way – by sword. We believe the assailant was on horseback and is an excellent swordsman.'

Lady Harrietta looked deliberately bemused.

'Why do you suspect my nephew Pim?'

'We have interviewed and eliminated all potential suspects and the only one we have yet to talk to is Pim de Vries.'

Lady Harrietta's expression changed in a blink; she looked livid.

'I am aware of the total disrespect your Uncle Albert and cousin Hans showed my family when they unlawfully raided my brother's home.' She spat the words out for effect.

'We needed to conduct a thorough search, your Ladyship and Meneer de Vries was not cooperating.'

'And what of the women?' she asked.

He stared at her dumbstruck.

'The women?' he repeated.

'Many women are equally skilled at riding and swordsmanship. I was taught from an early age and can probably give *you* a good beating. I know how badly trained soldiers are at fencing.'

General Stanley burst out laughing.

Harrietta turned on him.

'This is no laughing matter, General. This soldier has come into our house, our land and *our* country; making accusations about my nephew with no solid evidence, apart from his rather sloppy process of elimination.'

She was standing over Carl by now and the young officer had not prepared for this. He felt himself floundering.

'Well, what about the women?' she repeated. 'Why do you suspect these atrocious murders have been committed by a man?' She hesitated to let this sink in. 'I am not pointing the finger at anyone in particular but I could name eight, maybe ten ladies at home in Leeuwarden who could easily have committed these awful crimes.'

Carl sat there in silence.

'In reality, *you* are here under false pretences, spying in makeshift hides in our grounds – which, by the way, is trespassing – and listening to village gossip in our tavern.'

She paused.

'In Flintshire, my husband and I own the county and every dwelling inside it. We employ all the people to work on the estate, so you are also trespassing on our property by being here. I could ask the General to arrest you for espionage, and that carries a death sentence, Lieutenant.'

General Stanley thought she was incredible.

'I think this is your cue to leave and go back to Holland, Lieutenant, or I will have you arrested.' General Stanley rose to his feet and opened the French doors to the hall, where James Howell stood with the large oak entrance door open.

Carl stood, bowed briefly, and left without saying another word.

They watched him mount his horse and gallop down the long tree-lined drive towards the gates.

Tobias was seated at the gates, musket loaded and aimed at Carl as his horse sped through the gates.

'See to it that he leaves the tavern and follow him to the Humber,' she instructed as the General left. He nodded, puffed up with a whole new respect for Harrietta Bankes.

Pim and Gionne pulled Anouk and Viggo up and stood in the shadow of an old oak tree in the parkland grounds to watch Carl Leijtens gallop away, followed shortly afterwards by the General.

Minutes later, Tobias doffed his cap to them as he walked away into the woods, musket over his shoulder.

They rode quickly to the Hall to find out what had happened.

'You're back early. How were Bernard and Louise?' Lady Harrietta asked as they sat down for a late lunch that had been prepared by Mrs Pottage.

'They were delighted to see us, albeit briefly. They had another luncheon engagement, so we couldn't detain them,' Pim answered.

'And what of the lieutenant?' asked Gionne, impatient to know what had happened.

'I don't think he will trouble us again, my dear. I sent him back to Leeuwarden with a flea in his ear,' she laughed.

'How do we know he will go?' asked Gionne.

'The General is having him followed to the docks at Hull and will ensure he boards a ship bound for Holland.'

♦♦♦

Carl was furious and embarrassed. How dare she humiliate him in front of that drunkard who's a disgrace to his title?

He arrived at the tavern and collected his saddlebags, paid coin for his board and lodgings and left Flintwell, heading north. Even though he knew he was being followed – the man following made no effort to disguise his role – he had no intention of returning to Holland to meet his uncle's wrath.

At the port of Barton, he found a tavern and paid for a room.

He watched the man who'd followed him standing by the stables with his horse. It was dusk, so Carl discreetly came behind the man and slit his throat with a blade, hiding his body under straw bales in the stables and using the hay to clean away the blood.

He would eat in the tavern and take a flagon of beer to his room to plan his next move.

Furious as he was about his meeting with Lady Bankes, one thing she'd said stayed with him: it was interesting that his uncle and Hans had never considered a woman committing the crimes. Could Gionne possibly be the murderer? Was she being protected by Pim and his powerful aunt?

It would look good if he brought them both back to stand trial for the murders.

But how to trap them?

Could he tempt them to come north, or find them ambling through the countryside? Surely, they would relax their guard if they thought he had returned to Holland. He had the element of surprise on his side.

The more he drank the awful ale, the more he reflected on what Lady Harrietta had said to him. He was insulted by her insinuations: he was one of the top swordsmen in his regiment!

'No woman could ever defeat me!' he shouted aloud in his increasingly drunken state.

The next morning, Carl realised that the body of the man who'd followed him would soon be discovered. He must be miles away when it was as he was bound to be the first person they would seek out. He decided to try and find a secure hideaway near Failsworth Hall as this seemed to be close enough to the Flintwell estate without risk of being found. Who knows, he might even catch the young couple out riding, he mused.

As he rode towards Corringham village, the surrounding countryside became densely wooded. Finding a good hide would be easy enough. He wouldn't go to the village as this would raise suspicion and he presumed that the Bankes and Corringham's were friends or allies.

He was acutely aware of the gamekeepers however, and it occurred to him that in England they outnumbered the farmworkers – they seemed to be everywhere. That Tobias chap had a keen eye and a double-barrelled cap-lock hunting rifle; he assumed they were all equipped with similar rifles.

Carl had become familiar with the cap-lock guns as his unit had been recently re-armed with these; their flintlock guns were old and cumbersome especially in the wet.

He found a derelict barn by the roadside about a kilometre outside the village, and rested his horse inside, whist he climbed on what remained of the roof to keep lookout.

He had provisions – bread and preserved ham – and there was a nearby stream for fresh water.

Luckily, there was hay in the barn for his horse and he resolved that if he felt it was secure from prying eyes, he would camp here for the next couple of days.

CHAPTER NINE
Friesland

Messages took anything up to two weeks to arrive – longer if from abroad – and depending on how the message was sent, it didn't always arrive with the intended recipient. Families such as the de Vries would use a letterman to deliver messages personally, but for the majority of the populous it was an inexact science that lay in the hands of the lettermen and postal transport across the country, over to and from England.

And so it was that a letterman arrived at the farm outside Franeker. Janus was in the field whilst Lenje was tending the pigs, sheep and chickens in the stable yard.

The letterman's horse had been ridden hard and was grateful for the rest and fresh water supplied near the tethering post.

'Vrouw van't Kroenraedt?' he asked.

'Yes, that's me,' Lenje replied, smoothing a lock of her hair across her forehead as she stood.

'I have a message for you from England.' He handed her the thick, folded parchment paper with a seal on.

'Thank you. Please feed and water your horse before you leave,' she offered.

She looked at the message. It was Gionne's handwriting, but the seal was not recognisable. Impressive and bold, it had a crest on it and a coat of arms.

She knew Janus would have seen the rider arrive so he would be back from the fields soon.

She had never received a message like this before and resisted the temptation to break the seal and read its contents. Janus was her husband, and it was his right to do the honours.

As predicted, Janus came rushing in from the fields, his hands muddy.

'What did he want?' he demanded, washing his hands in the trough.

'It's a message from Gionne!' she said excitedly.

She handed it to Janus, who inspected the impressive seal, broke it and opened up the long letter in Gionne's beautiful handwriting. There was a second, shorter one but he was eager to read his daughter's words.

He read it in silence, his face reddening and his cheeks starting to puff out in anger.

'No! She can't do this to us!' he shouted, handing the letter to Lenje.

Lenje read it, quickly at first, then more slowly as her husband paced around the yard striking anything in his way.

Lenje tried to calm him: 'Come inside and let's read this slowly. There is a considerable amount of information here. Our daughter has reached out to us and it sounds like young Pim de Vries is simply trying to protect her.'

Janus had thunder in his eyes.

'That Protestant family is no good!'

'*Please* Janus,' Lenje begged.

Dear Mama and Papa,

I am safe. I have arrived in England at the home of Pim's aunt who is now Lady Harrietta Bankes, the Marchioness of Flintshire.

They are wonderful people and have welcomed us both into their family and protection, so we feel safe here.

We had to leave Frisia. I cannot explain to you why as you would be disappointed in me. All I can say is that Pim is innocent.

We have told Aunt Harrietta everything and she and Lord Bankes are being very supportive.

The journey was perilous, but we made it here with Anouk, Viggo – Pim's horse – and Bea. We think we are being followed by one of Major General Albert Leijtens men.

As your daughter, I love you both and respect everything you have done to raise me properly. I am a good Catholic girl and will be truthful to my religion. I want you to know that Pim and I love each other and wish, no, beg for your blessings when we marry. I promise that as a de Vries, I will maintain my Catholic religion, which I am able to do here in England.

Please be happy for us. I know you will be disappointed and angry with me for running away, but I had no choice. The less you know, the better. All I can say is that if the Major General had his way, innocent or not, Pim would hang and bring untold disrepute on our families. We did not want that.

Please find it in your hearts to forgive me.

I will love you forever.

Your loving daughter,

Gionne.

PS: Harrietta suggests you burn this letter after reading it.

They sat at the table and took turns re-reading it over several times. Each time they read the letter it prompted different questions.

What Janus could not come to terms with was the idea that she was to marry a de Vries – a Protestant family.

'There is nothing we can do, Janus,' Lenje said sadly. 'I am grateful she wrote to us. We know she is safe and living with a good family in England. Now we should destroy this letter before someone else finds it.'

She threw it on the fire before Janus could object.

They watched the parchment catch fire and disappear in flames.

'What about the second letter?' asked Lenje.

Janus retrieved the folded parchment from his pocket and looked again at the impressive seal with its coat of arms.

He opened it, read it quickly then handed it to Lenje.

'The fancy Lord Bankes is inviting us to attend our own daughter's wedding,' he said angrily. 'Does he think we are made of money and can just hop on a ship to England. What about the farm? We would be gone at least two weeks.'

He paced the room in an angry state.

♦♦♦

Thankful for the water and hay for his horse, the messenger from Lord Bankes spurred his horse on to his next destination.

It took a day to reach the de Vries estate and arriving late at night aroused suspicion from the staff at the impressive Landhuis.

The messenger dismounted and explained in English that he needed to personally hand a message from Lord Henry Bankes, the Marquis of Flintshire, to Pieter de Vries.

One of the servants could understand a little English and asked him to wait in the hall whilst he went to announce his arrival.

Minutes later, both Pieter and Maritje came quickly down the long corridor to the hall to meet him.

'I am Pieter de Vries, and this is my wife Maritje. You have a message for us?' he asked in very broken English.

'Yes, your Lordship. One from Lord Henry Bankes and his wife Harrietta and one from Pim de Vries.'

He handed them over.

'Have you ridden all the way from England?' asked Maritje.

'Apart from the sailing, yes maam. I am Lord Bankes' personal messenger.'

'Then you must rest here the night. We may have a message to return with you, if we may?' she asked.

'Certainly, maam and thank you. I apologise for the late arrival. I would have been here earlier if I'd found the farm in Friesland sooner. It was in the middle of nowhere,' he laughed.

'Oh? Who did you deliver a message to?' Pieter asked.

'It was to a Mr & Mrs van't Kroenraedt, on a farm north of Franeker.'

'That would have been Gionne's family,' Maritje remarked.

She asked one of the servants to take the messenger to the kitchens, find a bed for him and ask the stable boys to look after his horse.

'Thank you for coming all this way.' She took the messages from Pieter's hand and walked quickly back to their family room.

Pieter opened the message from Lord Henry Bankes first as Maritje opened Pim's letter and read it. She gave a squeal of excitement and stood up.

'They are to be married, Pieter!'

'Yes, and Lord Bankes has invited us to stay at his Landhuis for the wedding,' he answered, referring to the letter he held.

'I am concerned that Albert Leijtens has overstepped his authority and had Pim and Gionne followed to England. I understand from Henry that Carl Leijtens had the audacity to demand Pim return to Holland to stand trial on a jumped-up charge. He sent Leijtens away with a flea in his ear and had him followed to the port.'

Pieter was furious with this news and started to think about the powers he had to control Albert Leijtens. He would need to report the Major General's behaviour to his friends in the Dutch parliament.

Maritje sat at her desk and wrote a letter.
Then she wrote another.
'I think you should respond to Lord Bankes' invitation, Pieter. I have written to Pim and Gionne.'

The next morning Maritje asked the letterman if he could very kindly stop off at the remote farm on his way back and drop a letter off. She rewarded him handsomely with gold coins. He left with the three messages, grinning broadly.

♦♦♦

Major General Albert Leijtens was holding a meeting with his senior officers and the recently demoted Hendricks, when a lower ranked officer quietly came in through the door and handed Hans a note.

'What is it? Why have we this interruption?' Major General Leijtens demanded grouchily.

'It appears that there is a foreign letterman, delivering messages to the de Vries. He is thought to be English from his appearance and his horse,' Hans answered.

'Why has he been given free passage to cross our county?' Albert Leijtens barked.

Everyone sat in silence.

'Has no one intercepted him or his messages? They could relate to our wanted criminals.' His neck had reddened as it did when he was angry.

'Lieutenant Yacub, take four good men and arrest him,' he ordered. He stood saluted and left the room.

A few moments later they heard the sound of horses galloping out of the barracks.

Unbeknown to the young Lieutenant, all of Lord Bankes' lettermen were ex-British Army cavalry officers who had seen active service and were very skilled at killing people.

The letterman was on his guard as he approached the lonely farmhouse once again to deliver his first message. Again, he accepted some food and water, along with a baguette filled with ham and cheese for his onward journey.

He had instructions to report to Maarten de Vries in the port of Delfzijl to take one of his ships to Hull.

As he cantered along the coastal road to the port, he noticed a troop of five soldiers blocking the road ahead.

The officer with all the feathers and medals in his breast armour said something to him in Dutch.

He pulled up a short distance away, giving himself escape options.

'Sorry, I don't speak Dutch. I am here on official business from Lord Bankes, the Marquis of Flintshire. Please let me pass.'

In very broken English, Lieutenant Yacub said, 'You come with us,' and drew his sword.

There was a standoff as the letterman sized up his odds against five soldiers. He walked his horse to the left, and then to the right to see what reaction he got. He hoped that they were young untrained soldiers who had never been in battle.

'Allow me to pass,' he said again.

They hesitated at first and then walked their horses towards him. He tied the reins on the pommel of his saddle and drew his sword and dagger, prepared to defend himself as he had done many times before.

As they approached, he kicked his horse into a gallop and rushed into them, running his sword into the soldier to his left and his dagger into one on the right, instantly killing one of them. He used the pommel of his sword to knock the third out of his saddle, winding him as he fell on a rock, and barged his horse straight into the fourth soldier causing his horse to rear up.

He galloped away, as the young lieutenant, not quick enough to stop him, ordered the one soldier remaining on horseback to join him in pursuing the messenger.

The two gave chase. Their horses were fresher than the letterman's, so he decided to dismount and take them on foot.

He stood in the middle of the road as his horse obediently walked away into a field.

As the two approached on their horses, one soldier tried to run the letterman through, but he was too quick and stabbed the soldier in the leg, cutting off the stirrup leather at the same time, causing the soldier to fall off his horse.

Lieutenant Yacub pulled up and dismounted.

'You don't want to do this, son,' the letterman warned.

'It is my duty to arrest you,' said young Yacub.

The letterman stood with his sword in one hand and dagger in the other.

'I am an ex British Army officer, skilled at killing after too many wars, so please let me pass.'

Yacub thrust a parry at the letterman who side stepped, running the young pup's unprotected shoulder through, leaving his fighting arm useless.

The letterman whistled to his horse. It trotted over obediently and he mounted.

'Best if you return to barracks, Lieutenant, and tell your boss you were outnumbered.' He turned in his saddle and saluted, before galloping off towards the port of Delfzijl.

♦♦♦

Lenje read the letter from Maritje de Vries and smiled.

Janus asked whom the message was from.

'We are invited to meet with the de Vries next week. They will send a coach to pick us up. They wish to discuss the news they have also received about Gionne and Pim's betrothal.'

'I'm not going,' he said defiantly.

'Don't be absurd Janus! They may have the same concerns we have. It will be good to go – and to dress up,' she said.

'Who will look after the farm for two days whilst we are gone?'

'Oh, Vrouw de Vries is sending three of their farm workers to work for us whilst we are away.'

'They've thought of everything,' he said sarcastically.

'Yes, it's wonderful!' Lenje was thrilled.

♦♦♦

Two days before Janus and Lenje were due to be collected, three men arrived on horseback.

'We're here to help on the farm. We have come early to take instructions, Meneer,' the leader of the men said.

'Have you experience of our type of farming?' Janus asked sceptically.

'Oh yes. We looked at your land on the way over to see the crops you have as well as the animals. Can we show you?'

Janus followed them into the field.

Lenje made up bedding in the stables for them and made an extra-large pot of lamb stew.

Two days later a large coach arrived pulled by four horses. It was too big to fit in the small yard. The footmen carried out the one large case and placed it on the back of the coach. Both Janus and Lenje were in their only 'best' clothes. Even the coachmen's bright uniforms cost more than their clothes. They felt as if they were not good enough, which made them both nervous, as they had never met real aristocracy before. Janus had dealt with townsfolk, mayors and the relatively wealthy in their area, but never anyone of the de Vries' wealth and standing.

The journey took all day and the couple gazed at the passing countryside they had never seen before. The coach stopped several times to feed and water the horses and Janus and Lenje were given a small food hamper with a fine bottle of wine to enjoy.

As dusk approached, the coach turned through a stone gateway, where black ironwork was topped with gold. A long tree-lined driveway led impressively up to a huge imposing Dutch-style castle, where several people awaited them.

As the coach drew to a halt, a liveried footman jumped down, opened the carriage door and pulled out the steps.

Janus was the first to disembark and he held his hand out for Lenje.

'Welcome to our humble home!' A very distinguished man in his late fifties greeted them. Next to him was a very elegant lady in exquisite clothes. She smiled and held out her hand to Lenje.

'I am Maritje. Welcome to our home, Lenje,' she said informally.

'Yes, indeed! I am Pieter de Vries, and you are most welcome. I hope the journey was not too arduous and our coachmen look after your needs?'

They were spellbound. Not only by the welcome but the sheer size of their house. It was enormous.

They followed their hosts into a hall that had a wide stone staircase either side sweeping upstairs. They went through into an oak-panelled, carpeted room lined with antique, framed pictures of past relatives. Although large, it was still cosy and was evidently the family room.

They were asked to sit and offered a drink of porter.

'Your baggage will be sent up to your rooms in the west wing of the house,' a uniformed butler announced.

'We have arranged a little supper, so I hope you are hungry,' Maritje said.

Then the real conversation began and both couples were instantly drawn to each other. It was as if they had been friends for life.

An hour later, they sat around a table in an anteroom off the family room and served a four-course meal, the likes of which, neither Janus nor Lenje had ever experienced before.

'I'm sorry, Maritje, but we are simple farming folk and not used to all this,' Lenje said.

Maritje smiled warmly and held Lenje's hand.

'We are also farming people, Lenje, so please don't be overwhelmed by all this.' She gestured at the food and their surroundings.

'We are just delighted to finally meet Gionne's very clever mother, who taught her so much.'

Lenje was surprised and flattered.

'So … are you for or against this marriage?' asked Janus, broaching the subject.

'My sister is married to Henry Bankes and has the grant title of Marchioness of Flintshire. She is the one promoting the marriage,' Pieter said diplomatically.

Maritje, her hand still on Lenje's took over: 'As you know, we were delighted to have Gionne stay with us last summer with Truus and Pim. She is a real credit to you both and we love her dearly. Pieter and I are delighted and unsurprised by the announcement.'

Janus cleared his throat nervously. 'Can we speak candidly?' he asked.

Pieter waved a hand in assent.

'As you are aware, we are Catholics, and we had high hopes of our daughter marrying a Catholic suitor.'

Janus laughed at the sound of the words: 'I sound like a religious zealot!'

'Not at all, Janus.' Pieter leaned forward in his chair. 'Should we allow a small religious difference to get in the way of love? I would be surprised – and disappointed – if Gionne didn't hold onto her religion, as would Pim. The English have a marriage ceremony that would accommodate both religions, we are assured by Harrietta, my sister.'

Maritje nodded solemnly.

'You must be extremely proud of your beautiful daughter. Gionne knows her own mind and will challenge anyone who tries to change it. I would not concern yourself with religion. You have both brought her up well and we are delighted to welcome her and you into our family,' Maritje said holding Lenje's hand.

'On the subject of the wedding, Henry and Harrietta have invited us all to stay at Flintwell Hall, and you will be our guests on the journey there.'

Pieter held his hand up as Janus began to protest.

'Our carriage will collect you and you'll meet us at Delfzijl, from where the family operates ships around the world. My brother will secure bunks on board their Hull-bound ship. Henry is sending a carriage to meet us. It's all arranged.'

'That is so very kind of you, but we will be unable to go – we cannot leave our farm for that length of time,' Janus said sadly.

'It's all taken care of, Janus. The three men we sent to you are from our arable farm – they will look after your crops and livestock, doing all that is needed,' Pieter said pouring more wine.

'We can't afford to pay people to work on our farm,' Janus said, panicking slightly.

'No matter. These men are under my employment, and they will work where we want them. They are also ex-soldiers so will provide protection as well. Let's not hear another word.' Pieter was final.

Janus sat back to take it all in. De Vries' commercial and business command was impressive.

After the sumptuous meal, Maritje took Lenje on a tour of the house, and Janus settled into the comfiest chair he had ever sat in to enjoy a large glass of port with Pieter.

They talked about politics, the de Vries family and local news.

Janus was overwhelmed but happy to be in the company of such a gentleman. He soon relaxed and was talking about his farm and the local politics in Franeker.

♦♦♦

Gossip spread around Franeker and Leeuwarden of a mounted horseman taking out a troop of five soldiers single handedly. There were too many witnesses for the rumour to be quashed.

Major General Albert Leijtens was furious, to say the least.

He demanded to see Hans, Hendricks, and the injured Yacub immediately.

The bodies of the two soldiers were brought back to barracks along with the horses and the wounded Yacub and two other soldiers, all of whom had received medical attention on the roadside.

'Lieutenant Yacub will live. The soldier who ran him through knew what he was doing as the blade penetrated just centimetres from his body armour and went through his shoulder joint, disarming him,' Hans said to the collected officers in front of the Major General.

'To be able to kill two of my best soldiers and wound you, Yacub and two others, he must have been a professional,' Hans added.

'Do we know anything about him?' asked Hendricks. 'Where he came from, and to whom he delivered messages?'

'That's obvious,' snarled the Major General. 'The letters were to de Vries and those farmers. Messages about the fugitives we seek.'

'He went to see Maarten de Vries then sailed to Hull this morning, Major General,' one of the aides piped up.

'We must find out what was in those messages.' Albert Leijtens was obsessed.

'With respect, Father, we have no jurisdiction here.' Hans objected, taking his life into his hands.

The Major General rounded on him, 'I am your commanding officer here, not your father, and who are you to lecture me on jurisdiction? I am the law here!' he bellowed.

'I am sorry to interrupt, Major General,' Hendricks said meekly. 'But on a point of civil law, he is right: we have no jurisdiction to intervene with private messages.'

Albert Leijtens puffed himself up.

'If you are all so bloody clever, what can we do? Two of our soldiers are dead, and three are wounded including one officer. Who is going to make reprimands here? And don't tell me the British Army!' he bellowed.

Everyone was quiet.

'Any news from Lieutenant Carl Leijtens?' he asked.

'Nothing as yet sir,' answered the aide.

'Saddle my horse. I'm going to pay Pieter de Vries a visit.'

'Unannounced, Major General? Is that wise?' Hans challenged his father again but the challenge went unheeded.

♦♦♦

Major General Albert Leijtens galloped up the long drive to the de Vries Landhuis with five officers following. He dismounted and banged on the front door.

They knew he was coming as one of the gamekeepers had run to tell the head butler.

Pieter gave firm instructions to make the Major General wait on the doorstep.

Finally, after a time, the Head Butler opened the door.

'Major General Leijtens.' He bowed formally. 'Are you expected?' The servant adopted the most stiff, arrogant pose he could.

'I demand to see Pieter de Vries on official business, and I *don't* care to be kept waiting.'

'Please wait here and I will try to locate Meneer de Vries.'

He closed the door on the Major General, much to his fury, making him wait on the doorstep.

'Show him into my study,' Pieter instructed. 'But ask my land manager Yan to join me first.'

By this time, the Major General was well out of sorts.

He stomped into Pieter's study with another officer in tow.

'This is an unexpected visit Major General. I hope it is important, considering you have burst into my home unannounced.' Pieter sat at his large glass desk with his land manager seated to one side.

'Two of my men have been killed and three officers seriously wounded by a letterman, whom we understand came to see you and the van't Kroenraedt's at their farm.'

Pieter de Vries looked unperturbed.

'That was clumsy. Where and when did this happen? Did you wish me to take this up politically?'

He purposefully did not invite the Major General to sit.

'Clumsy?' He raged. 'He was en route from the farm in Franeker to the port of Delfzijl where he boarded one of your ships back to England.'

'Are you telling me that five of your best soldiers were taken out by one sole English letterman on horseback?' De Vries sounded incredulous.

This made the Major General even angrier and his neck reddened under his pompous uniform.

'If the letterman was on his way to the port of Delfzijl from the direction of Franeker, why did your men want to stop him? Was there something suspicious about him? On what grounds did your officer in command decide to stop him? I believe our laws dictate they should have the freedom to pass?'

Albert Leijtens was caught off guard. De Vries' accurate reference to the law made him colour further.

'We had reason to believe the British horseman was a spy,' he said, desperately. 'Nonsense! If he had been to deliver messages to us – and I am not confirming he did – and then to the farmers in Franeker, what made your officer think he was a spy?'

The Major General shifted from one foot to the other, clearly unhappy, but he would not be moved.

'I demand to know who the messages were from and what they contained as I conclude they were from wanted criminals.'

'You may demand all you like, Major General! As you are very much aware, these were *private* messages, and you have no jurisdiction here.' Pieter sat calmly, crossed his legs and looked at the Major General.

He stood his ground but Pieter could see sweat beading on his forehead.

'I also take issue with your insinuation that my son Pim and his fiancée Gionne – if that is whom you are referring to – are criminals. Do we not have a rule here that everyone is innocent until proven guilty? And as I understand it, you have no proof, do you, Major General?'

'They are wanted for questioning relating to the vagrant murders,' the Major General asserted.

'So ... *not* wanted criminals?' Pieter drove the point home.

He stood up and walked over to the Major General, who was slightly shorter and more rotund than him.

'I would strongly suggest that you conclude your investigations on the basis that the culprit could not be found. If it happens again then we should re-visit your evidence.'

The Major General stood silent.

'If that is everything, Leijtens, I have important state business to conclude. Good day to you.'

The door to the study suddenly opened and the butler ushered the Major General and his aide out through the hall and closed the main door behind them.

Leijtens was fuming; Pieter De Vries had embarrassed him in front of his officers.

They galloped away back to barracks.

♦♦♦

A week later a few miles outside of Leeuwarden, another vagrant was found dead in the drainage canal, a wound through his heart.

CHAPTER TEN
England

The body of a man was found under bales of straw three days later, and a message was sent to the High Sheriff when someone recognised him as one of Stanley's men.

An investigation to find out if the Dutchman had indeed returned to Holland proved futile. It was assumed that he was still in the vicinity and Lord Henry and Lady Harrietta were informed.

♦♦♦

Carl had found an ideal hiding place: his hide was a deep hole he had dug into the soft earth and covered over with a latticework of tree branches and foliage. No one would ever find him.

He foraged at night and stole food and provisions from the local villagers, disappearing deep into the woods after each raid.

The disused barn he'd originally found, he quickly realised, was used by locals for amorous pursuits, with locals using the tree stump outside on which to fornicate. On one grim occasion, he'd had to endure several hours of a local prostitute working her day, with a string of men she 'entertained' on the creaky old bed and stained straw mattress. After each tryst, she used a bowl of dirty water to wash herself. The grimy liquid dripped on him as he lay only feet away under a blanket in the cellar, hoping desperately that the floor was strong enough to hold the bed. He was relieved when, at long last, she ran out of customers and he watched her counting her coins as she sat on the bed.

He left that night to find a less unsavoury and more secure hiding place.

His new hiding place was much more secure in fact, as the forest was vast and swathes of it little used. Carl felt that some time needed to pass before he could resume pursuit of his quarry.

His beard by now was long and bushy, and his clothes were in tatters, so he stole some off a washing line.

He missed his home. He also missed the camaraderie of his fellow officers at the Leeuwarden army base. He was becoming very thin and was aware of malnutrition so he tried to keep healthy.

Thankfully, the weather had been usually mild with little rain, so he was at least dry.

His horse was left in a field with other horses to graze, his saddle and uniform buried under woodland growth nearby.

Carl ventured out at night to walk the hour it took through the woods until he arrived at a clearing where he could see into the Failsworth Estate using his telescope. In time, he felt sure he would see his quarries.

♦♦♦

Lord and Lady Bankes were visiting Sir Bernard and Lady Louise on a matter of estate business, they told Pim and Gionne.

Assembled in their drawing room at Failsworth Hall, were General Stanley, Randulph Blake

(Flintwell Hall estate steward) and the Failsworth Hall gamekeepers.

'Thank you, Bernard for hosting this meeting. We wanted to keep it away from Flintwell Hall for obvious reasons,' Henry began.

General Stanley, looking cleaner and more well-kempt than usual, cleared his throat: 'We found the body of our scout in the tavern stables in Barton, throat cut, begging your pardon, ladies,' he said.

'And we cannot ascertain for sure that the Dutchman boarded a ship to Holland, so we must assume he is still here.'

'I agree, my Lords,' injected Randulph Blake. 'Our gamekeepers have found evidence someone was hiding out in an old barn just outside Corringham village, but he must have left there some time ago.'

One of Sir Bernard's gamekeepers rocked from foot to foot.

'If you have something to say, young man, please feel free to speak. The more information we have, the better we are,' said Sir Bernard.

'Your Lordships and my Ladies,' said a very nervous gamekeeper, 'I were checking fox traps int' north woods beyond the lake, bordering his Lordship's land. There be someone there as traps had been used.'

'Thank you, my man,' said Bernard.' We need to search that area thoroughly.'

The other gamekeeper put his hand up, like a child in school.

'Well?' asked Randulph.

'There is a strange horse in the south woods, and it's not one of the wild ponies we have. Looks like it's been abandoned by cavalry,' he said.

'This is all very disconcerting,' Louise Failsworth said. 'We must find this man before he does more harm.'

'We will, maam,' said General Stanley.

♦♦♦

The search for the Dutch lieutenant was started in earnest the following day with a hunting party made up by Stanley's men, and gamekeepers from both estates.

They used bloodhounds and beaters, as if hunting game, but this was part of their plan to avert suspicion from prying eyes.

♦♦♦

Carl was curled up into a tight ball, half asleep when he heard the beaters, banging drums and thrashing the ground. At first, he was confused until he heard the dogs barking. *English bloodhounds*, he decided from their distinctive, deep bark. He had come across them on exercises last year with the English army.

He had to leave his hiding place and quickly. He estimated they were several miles away but coming in his direction.

The dogs would find him for sure, but there were two options for escape routes: One was up a tree as high as he could go; the other was to head south, through the Flintwell Estate into the next county.

Carl gathered his small belongings, his sword and dagger and left his hideaway, heading south.

♦♦♦

Sure enough, and not long after he'd left, the hounds found his hide. The men searched every inch of the deep hole for any clues.

'He's been here a while, General,' said one of the gamekeepers.'

'I would say he heard the hounds and went south, by the looks of these tracks,' said another.

'Let's go then.' Stanley was on his horse, with Sir Bernard Failsworth at his side to oversee the hunt.

They followed the trail, hounds leading until they came upon the lake that bordered both estates.

'As a soldier, he would either swim across or use the water's edge to hide his scent from the dogs,' Randulph said.

'It's a long way to swim,' pointed out a gamekeeper.

They all stood there, rather disconsolate. Sir Bernard sensed the mood and issued instructions.

'It's getting late. Stanley, post several men around the lake as guards tonight. We can pick this up tomorrow. He can't be far away.'

'Yes, Sire.'

♦♦♦

And Sir Bernard was right. Carl Leijtens was at the water's edge, hiding in the reed bed and holding a reed tube to his mouth so he could breathe as he sank under the water, just feet from where they were all standing.

It was cold, but he didn't have to wait long before darkness fell. He could get past these idiots easily and return to his hide – the one place he was certain they would not revisit.

Eight men surrounded the lake, and each walked a set path along its edge, which he timed at ten minutes. There were no dogs, which was a big mistake but good news for him.

Carl waited until the nearest guard had passed his hiding area in the reeds and slid out of the water as quietly as he could. Crawling on hands and knees, he waited until he reached the long meadow grass, then the trees before he stood up and disappeared into the dark woods.

He was shivering and needed to get out of his wet clothes. Hopefully the clothes he'd stolen would still be in his pit.

Mindful of the gamekeepers from both estates, he stealthily made his way back, reaching the cover just before dawn.

Thankfully, no one had bothered to take his things, and he found the clothes he was looking for. Wrapped up in two horse blankets, and desperate to get his blood circulating again, he soon fell asleep.

He woke to the sounds of hounds barking and the thunder of horses' hooves, as the search party went past a short distance away. He prayed that the hounds wouldn't pick up his scent, and they didn't.

This was not a safe hideaway anymore; tonight he would find somewhere new, closer to the Failsworth Estate.

In his mind, he kept asking himself what his uncle Major General Leijtens would want him to do. Arresting the two runaways and escorting them on a day's ride to Hull docks, and then on a ship to Holland, would be difficult. Uncle Albert was convinced Pim de Vries was guilty of the murders, so challenging him to a duel to the death would be seen as justice.

But what about the girl? Carl mused. Uncle Albert wanted them both but he couldn't challenge *her* to a duel – it was not done to fight a lady.

That night, after stealth walking for several hours back to the lake, he found an ideal hideaway and lookout point.

CHAPTER ELEVEN
Events in Flintshire

The letterman arrived back from Holland and reported to Lord Bankes. They were taking high tea with Pim and Gionne, and Lady Failsworth was there as well.

'Sire, here are three messages from Holland,' the letterman said.

'Good grief man, you look as if you've had a rough ride!' Henry gestured at his torn, blood-stained uniform and bedraggled look.

'My Lord, I did encounter some resistance,' he said briefly.

'Oh? Tell more,' Harrietta probed.

He cleared his throat.

'There was a troop of five cavalry men, one of whom demanded I had over these messages. I was on my way from the farm in Franeker to Delfzijl. They drew their swords. I asked several times for them to let me pass on the letterman code but the young lieutenant said he wanted to see what the messages were about. I told him that they were private – for you, my Lord. They started to charge and I did what I had to.'

'And what was that?' asked Harrietta.

He coughed and stood up straighter.

'I ran one through with my sword, stabbed one in the leg, kicked two off their mounts and pegged the lieutenant through the shoulder.'

'Not much gets past you, eh George?' stated Henry.

'No, my Lord, they were a disgrace to the Dutch Cavalry in my opinion. Green and inexperienced.'

'So, you left a wake of destruction in my home country?' added Harrietta with a smile.

'Maam,' he said in assent.

'Very well done, George! There will be an extra coin for you this month. Go, eat, rest and repair.'

'Yes, my Lord and I thank you.' He bowed, saluted and marched out.

'Worth his weight in gold, that man,' Henry said admiringly. 'Best letterman we have. Ex cavalry officer in the Blues – the Royal Horse Guards.'

They opened their messages and read in silence.

Harrietta stood up and cried out.

'Yes! How wonderful!'

'Looks like both your parents are coming to your wedding,' Henry said to Pim and Gionne.

'How marvellous!' said Pim.

Gionne was reading her letter from her mother and started to weep.

Pim immediately went to her.

'What is it?

'Mama and Papa have given us their blessing for our wedding on the condition that I remain a faithful Catholic.'

'That's terrific news!' Pim hugged her.

'And more news,' added Harrietta. 'Your mother and father have met my brother and Maritje and got on so well that your parents will accompany them on the journey here. Gionne, we will ensure that they are happy with the ceremony.'

After the evening meal the ladies went to take tea and sherry in the library, whilst the men lit cigars and poured large schooners of porter.

'We need to fish out this Dutchman before the wedding. I'm uncomfortable knowing he is out there somewhere. He is a liability,' Lord Henry said between puffs on his glowing cigar.

'I have my estate manager and yours together with our gamekeepers and Stanley's men scouring the woodlands. We will find him. After all, he is now wanted for murder,' stated Sir Bernard.

'If I catch him, I will run him through with my sword,' said Pim bravely.

They all laughed.

'Well gentlemen, we have eight weeks until the wedding to find this Dutch killer and bring him to justice,' added Lord Henry.

♦♦♦

Preparations for the forthcoming wedding were well underway.

Gionne, Louise Failsworth and Harrietta became inseparable.

Pim and Gionne dined every night with Henry and Harrietta and, gradually, Henry realised what an asset Pim would be to the estate with his brilliant mind and financial savvy.

Pim looked at situations differently and would suggest alternatives to those put forward to Henry. The estate advisors saw Pim as a fresh set of eyes and quickly realised that if they wanted their plans to succeed, they would need to enlist his support.

Pim became very popular on the estate and in the local governance of Flintshire, as he accompanied Henry on rural meetings with men from London.

Gionne was also a powerful young lady, who would be hard to sway. She insisted on going to the estate chapel to receive the sacraments from a Catholic priest who rode up on a cart drawn by donkey from the monastery every week.

She, in turn, visited the Jesuit monks with fresh food and tales from home.

She practised her swordsmanship every other day in the orangery with one of General Stanley's lieutenants, who could never beat her, as well as with Pim in the flower garden watched by Henry and other staff.

She was bright, intelligent and knowledgeable about many things.

Her relationship with key members of staff built up solidly. With her grounding as a farmer's daughter, she never put on any airs and graces and saw the staff as her equals. They loved this about her.

One day, she sat in the kitchens with a cup of tea.

'Mrs Cribb, how long have you been head housekeeper here?'

'Oh maam, about thirty years. My mother and grandmother were head housekeepers, too.'

Mrs Pottage spoke: 'My lady, Mrs Cribb is married to James Howell the Head Butler, but tradition has it that as head housekeeper, she will always be called Mrs Cribb in honour of her ancestors.'

'You can talk!' Mrs Cribb laughed. 'Mrs Pottage has been here even longer. Born upstairs, she was, and her great grandmother was head cook.'

'Don't tell me your real name is not Mrs Pottage?' Gionne asked, enjoying this bonding.

'She's my mother, and married to Randulph Blake, my stepfather,' replied George Bedlan, the first footman, as he walked in on the conversation carrying a basketful of shoes to clean.

'You are such lovely people,' Gionne said warmly. 'And you'll all be involved in our wedding and come to the party, too.'

'Oh no, my lady! That will not be allowed by his Lordship,' said Mrs Pottage shaking her head.

'You leave Lord Henry to me,' Gionne giggled. 'And please drop the "my lady" or "maam." I am but a farmer's daughter, and always will be.'

'Only when you are on your own,' Mrs Cribb said. 'In the company of his Lordship, we must address you with respect.' 'Understood,' Gionne said. 'But I am simply Gionne when on my own, ok?'

Every day she would skip down into the servants' quarters and wish them all a good morning.

She took over the organisation of her wedding from Louise Failsworth, whilst including her and Harrietta in all the big decisions so they felt a part of it.

Both Louise and Harrietta quickly realised what an intelligent and capable young lady Gionne was and knew instantly that she and Pim would make a good match.

♦♦♦

One evening as they prepared to go to their bedchambers, Henry said, 'I am really impressed with young Pim. He has an intellect like no other.

He has already mastered the estate finances and shown me how and where to improve our yields off the fields and look for trade with other estate owners further afield. Even Bernard is impressed. I think we have found our successors, my dear.'

Harrietta smiled at her husband. She knew she could not give birth to an heir, and she loved Henry for his acceptance of this. Perhaps her nephew and his new bride would be perfect.

'I agree. And Gionne is his equal, both in intellect and how well she gets on with all the staff. They love her – and respect her too.'

Both had become increasingly worried about to whom to pass on the title of Marquis and Marchioness.

♦♦♦

A week later a Dutch letterman arrived with a message for Lord and Lady Bankes.

He was escorted into the library, where Henry and Harrietta were taking morning refreshments with Gionne and Pim and discussing the wedding arrangements.

Harrietta spoke to the letterman in Dutch:

'Thank you for bringing this message from home. Please refresh yourself, take quarters, which Howell will show you, and wait for a possible message to take back.'

He bowed.

'Howell, can you find this letterman a room to rest in, and ask Mrs Pottage to feed him well?'

'Yes, your Ladyship.'

Henry was already reading the message and laughed out loud.

'Well, well, well!' was all he said, before passing the message to his wife. Gionne and Pim were on the edge of their seats as Lady Harrietta skimmed through the letter.

'It appears that Albert Leijtens has accused you *both* of the vagrant murders and was sent away with a flea in his ear by your father, Pim.'

She paused for effect.

'Then, *another* vagrant was found dead on the road from Leeuwarden to your family estate, which rules you both out.'

Pim and Gionne sat stunned. In the space of seconds, they had been jointly accused and cleared of murder.

Lady Harrietta continued. 'Leijtens has always been resentful of our family's wealth and good fortune. I remember my brother telling me that at the academe, he was a bully.'

She reread the message again.

'Gionne, let's pen a message to Pieter and Maritje and they can pass it on to Janus and Lenje. We'll tell them about the Jesuits who will be attending the wedding.'

Gionne nodded enthusiastically.

Pim looked at his new mentor, Lord Henry.

'With this news of the killings continuing after we left, do you think we should somehow let Lieutenant Leijtens know, so he can come out of hiding and go home?'

'Very compassionate of you, Pim,' said Lord Henry. 'It's worth a try, though I suspect he will think it's a ploy to trick him. I believe he's too embedded in his mission to be distracted.'

'What if he was shown this message?'

'Let's talk to Stanley and Bernard and get their counsel,' Henry said, further admiring the young man's principles.

Harrietta was looking at the note in her hand and found one had attached itself to the back of it. It was addressed to Gionne.

'This is for you, my dear,' Harrietta said.

Gionne carefully opened the letter, instantly recognising the neat handwriting.

'It's from Truus!' she said, delighted.

She read it in silence, the expression on her face changing from delight to a frown, and then to laughter.

'Truus wants to come to our wedding and be my bridesmaid! That would be perfect. Can she?' Gionne asked everyone.

'Of course, Gionne! I will write to Pieter and ask him to send her ahead of the rest of the family so she can help us with the preparations.'

Harrietta was already two steps ahead; she suspected Truus was broken hearted when her best friend fell in love with her brother and they absconded.

Gionne immediately sat at the small desk and wrote Truus a long letter telling her all the news and how wonderful her aunt is. She suddenly realised that she may have inadvertently hurt her friend and resolved to make amends.

♦♦♦

Several days later, Henry had called a meeting in his study with General Stanley, his friend and mentor Sir Bernard, Randulph Blake, the estate steward, Sir Bernard's estate steward, Tobias Tilley, his head game keeper, and Pim.

'Gentlemen, we have a situation: the Dutchman is in hiding on our lands and is threatening harm to two of our guests. He believes that young Pim here has committed several murders and has been sent to arrest him and take him back for questioning. It has come to light that he is misinformed – there have been further incidents in Frisia that put our guests in the clear. We need to find a way of flushing him out unharmed and show him these messages.'

He waved two letters in his hand.

'We wish him no harm but want him to return to his country as soon as possible,' Sir Bernard added.

Lord Henry nodded and continued: 'The issue we have is that he believes he has a mission to fulfil. He will not believe anything we tell him, as he will be primed for tricks. Remember he is a trained soldier in the Dutch Cavalry. So ... any thoughts or ideas on how we flush him out?'

Tobis Tilley spoke up: 'My Lord, we know where some of his hides are. We could leave messages in Dutch for him to read. He seems to move on a regular basis. He is very adept at camouflage.'

'Flush the man out – don't give him a chance to run,' said General Stanley.

'That's not the point, Stanley,' Sir Bernard interjected. 'We mean him no harm. If he doesn't take the bait then we should try to find him by means of both hounds and beaters, as we would with game.'

Pim was silent, listening.

'What say you, Pim?' asked Lord Henry.

'Carl Leijtens is a determined man,' Pim said. 'He was two years above me at the academe and was the top of his class. His whole family are entrenched in soldiering. He has been well taught in all aspects of combat and is a master swordsman. So be careful if you do engage him.'

He walked around the room.

'I am with Sir Bernard. He will think it's a trick to flush him out. Even if he reads the messages, he'll assume they have been made up. The only way to get him to come out of hiding is to give myself up to him.'

Pim looked for a response.

'That's foolish!' Henry said.

'Not if Gionne and I went to look for him with Aunt Harrietta close nearby, to explain the latest news from home,' Pim said.

Lord Henry stood and spoke firmly: 'I will not put my wife, nor you and Gionne in that dangerous position.' He flushed with anger at the very suggestion.

Everyone was silent.

'Henry, to be honest, Pim has quite a good idea,' Sir Bernard said quietly. 'If we have enough men standing by no harm will come to Pim, Gionne or Harrietta.'

'I don't like it,' Henry said defiantly.

The door to the study opened with a creak and everyone turned to see who it was.

Harrietta walked slowly into the room and up to her husband. Everyone bowed in respect. She took his hand.

'Have you been eavesdropping, my dear?' Lord Henry asked.

'Yes, I have. This is a delicate situation and I have known Carl Leijtens and his cousin Hans since youth. He is a single-minded young man who is very loyal to his uncle and will be hard to persuade that he no longer needs to continue with his mission. Pim's suggestion is a good one, and I'd be happy to reassure young Carl, that we are not trying to trick him. I know we will be quite safe,' she said in her quiet voice with a slight Dutch accent.

Everyone in the study was nodding their agreement as his Lordship glanced around the room.

'This is preposterous,' reaffirmed Lord Henry. 'I think you are all mad!'

He paused, thinking.

'Very well, but I want a ring of your men, Stanley as well as our gamekeepers surrounding this man, in case he does anything stupid.'

Over the next week, the gamekeepers scoured the woodland, fields and old hides they were aware he had used, but Carl Leijtens was a master at undercover tactics. He covered his tracks well, and whilst the estate gamekeepers were some of the best in England, they admired his ability to thwart them.

They left messages in each of his hides written in both Dutch and English by Harrietta.

♦♦♦

Carl was getting used to the vagrant way of life. He was always cold, hungry and tired, but ever alert. His beard now reached his chest and his hair was greasy and riddled with lice. He knew he must stink to high heaven, which is why he took every opportunity for a midnight swim in the lake whenever he could. He was grateful for the intense undercover training he'd received from the army, when he volunteered to train in unarmed combat and jungle warfare, in case he was recruited to fight in the Dutch colonies overseas. This jungle training was now coming to the fore in helping him hide and spy on his quarry.

He often saw the gamekeepers and their bloodhounds pass within metres of where he was, but still he remained undetected.

Returning to some of his old hides, he found several notes but dismissed them as a ruse to trick him.

He worried about his horse, which they would have found by now, and moved every four hours so that they did not detect him. He also worried that he had not seen the young couple for some time now. He knew they were still at the hall because he would overhear conversations between staff, whenever he ventured close to the kitchens to steal food. Several times staff members spotted him but waved him away, assuming he was a tramp. He was lucky.

He desperately wanted to get a message to his uncle, the Major General or to Hans, to tell them he was alive and safe, and still on the mission he was sent on, but how?

He was grateful the weather was mild and, wrapped in blankets and a sheepskin he stole from the village, he covered himself in foliage and lay in the lair he had dug the previous night away from the lake.

Carl gazed up at the starlit night sky and thought about how much longer he would pursue his mission.

What if the messages were true and the vagrant killer was still at large in Frisia? I could give myself up, have a hot bath, shave, dress in clean clothes and eat a decent meal. Maybe even go home a hero, he thought to himself.

He thought about the letters, written in Harrietta's hand. He remembered her from when he was growing up: tall, dark hair, very attractive and friendly, unlike the rest of that family.

He seemed to remember that Pieter de Vries was at the academe in Leeuwarden with his Uncle Albert, before he left to go to a superior school in Amsterdam. There was certainly a lot of animosity between Uncle Albert and the de Vries family. Hans had told him some stories of the past.

What he couldn't understand was why Gionne van't Kroenraedt had got involved with the de Vries family. Her family were honest, hardworking farmers and Catholics. Why was Gionne with Pim de Vries?

He knew she was very bright, a bit of a tomboy, as well as an accomplished horsewoman and fencer by all accounts.

Uncle Albert was convinced that Pim de Vries had committed the vagrant murders and he remained his target.

Should he test the waters to see if these messages were true? And if so, how?

He could leave messages for them and suggest a meeting place with Harrietta Bankes, somewhere he could see who else was there, and decide if it was a trap.

He had to think of a suitable location to meet Harrietta and how to establish if she was telling the truth or not. It was all very risky.

Whilst hiding around the kitchens to steal food, he had picked up on a buzz of excitement from the staff at Failsworth Hall about the forthcoming wedding of the young couple. Surely not!

They were Dutch nationals and from opposite ends of the religious spectrum. How could this be allowed to happen? Carl was totally confused, not knowing what the right course of action was to take.

He resolved that he needed to apprehend Pim de Vries before their wedding.

A little later, back in his cold, damp hiding place he had more doubts: what if the notes *were* true and Pim was innocent. That might put him, a foreigner, in serious trouble.

What should he do?

♦♦♦

A letterman was riding towards the village of Failsworth and slowed to a trot to rest his horse as he neared his destination. It gave him time to look around at the beautiful countryside on this crisp morning. He had been riding hard throughout the night from London, carrying a message for Lord Corringham he knew was urgent.

His horse suddenly stopped and gave out a neigh, his hooves cropping at the ground.

The letterman looked into the ditch beside him and saw a figure lying there. He couldn't make out if it was male or female as the torso was covered by a vast cloak, and the head concealed by a large cavalier-style felt hat. He marked its position by building a small stone pyramid on the roadside and resolved to report it to the local High Sheriff's office.

He rode on towards Failsworth Hall where he diligently delivered his message to Lord Corringham's aide and asked to see the head butler, who gave him directions to Flintwell, where the High Sheriff's office was located.

'This is the third such killing, we have had in the area, and the target has always been vagrants or travellers,' General Stanley commented when told of the recent discovery.

'We must investigate this. I want several men on it,' he instructed his officers. This, on top of the situation with the Dutchman, was all he needed.

It never occurred to Clifford Stanley that what was happening in Flintshire bore any similarity to the events in Frisia that Carl Leijtens was investigating.

CHAPTER TWELVE

Wedding Preparations

Truus' arrival at Flintwell Hall was the source of huge excitement and joy for Gionne. The two friends embraced and held one another so long, Pim began to wonder if they would ever let go.

'I know I'm only your brother, Truus,' he laughed, 'but a greeting would be nice!'

The three of them laughed and Truus hugged her brother.

'Lovely to see you too, Pim,' she said, 'But what can I say? I've missed my dear best friend terribly.'

Gionne smiled and squeezed her friend's hand.

'And I you, Truus,' she said. 'I'm beyond thrilled that you're here. Come! I must introduce you to Aunt Harrietta. And Uncle Henry, of course.'

Pim chuckled as the two friends tore off up the great staircase. He could hear Gionne listing the staff Truus must meet, too.

'Then, of course, there's Mrs Cribbs … oh! And Mrs Pottage!'

The household staff under Mrs Cribb, were buzzing with excitement and kept very busy at Flintwell Hall with preparations for the guests from Holland and the wedding itself.

This was going to be massive – the biggest party that Lord and Lady Bankes had ever held – and they wanted perfection.

The entire north wing had been allocated to the de Vries and the van't Kroenraedt's. Gionne had been moved out of her apartment into a separate room near to where her parents would be in the north wing.

In the kitchens, Mrs Pottage had written up a massive list of food to feed the three hundred guests attending the wedding.

The food would be collected from the estate farms as well as markets in the local towns and villages.

Harrietta Bankes had asked Mrs Cribb and Mrs Pottage together with James Howell and George Bedlan, to organise the kitchen, scullery and above-stairs serving staff into teams with specific instructions.

Under Tobias Tilley, the gamekeepers were given the list of wild game required from the estate, including pheasant, partridge, pigeon, duck, and goose. A deer would be prepared for the table as well a few wild boars.

Flintwell Hall was built by the first Henry Bankes over 100 years previously and has been extended by each Lord Bankes since.

The current Henry Bankes – the 5th Marquis of Flintshire – added an impressive orangery following his visit to Italy and created a private garden surrounding it. Flintwell Hall stood prominent on the top of a small rise in the land, surrounded by a thousand acres of grassland, kept neat by grazing sheep, deer and cows. It was a majestic vision to anyone visiting for the first time.

The front's main entrance was through a colonnaded structure, under which a full four horse and carriage could enter, thereby screening passengers from inclement weather.

Around the rear of the hall stood the orangery and private gardens lined by neat privet hedges. These led to the maze, which was designed by Lady Antoinnette Bankes the 3rd Marchioness, as a discreet meeting place for her dalliances, whilst her older husband was in London. Around the maze were a number of love-seat alcoves where one could spend a romantic time unseen by prying eyes.

Harrietta thought it hilarious that this had gone on all those years ago and loved the history and mystery of it all.

A team of groundsmen worked on the gardens surrounding the Hall so they were in perfect condition for the guests to enjoy, especially the famous maze, which took a lot of time to keep neatly trimmed.

In Flintwell village, all the inhabitants were also buzzing with excitement as Lady Harrietta had recruited most of the ladies for service work. It would mean more coin for them as most of the men folk were employed in the grounds.

A huge marquee was being built on the lawns next to the orangery, where the wedding breakfast would be served to the invited guests.

Lady Harrietta had come across these tents in Holland and France, where they were often used by military officers to distinguish them from those used by soldiers.

Randulph Blake together with James Howell was supervising the creation of this marquee. It was built from wooden poles, secured by ropes to long heavy iron nails hammered into the ground, and covered in sail canvas. A linen canopy lined the interior under the sail roof. The floor was made from wooden ships' planks bought from the shipbuilders in Hull along with rolls of waxed sailcloth which would cover the structure.

It was hoped that the day of the wedding would be dry, bright and sunny.

Lady Harrietta kept a close eye on everything under stairs and in the grounds for the wedding preparation.

It was going to be an impressive event, to which Lord and Lady Bankes would be able to invite all the local nobility as well as prominent guests from London. It would be the social event of the year in the east of England.

◆◆◆

In Holland, a carriage pulled up outside Janus and Lenje's farm to collect them. Their travelling trunks, containing all their clothes and personal items, had been collected several days before and were well on their way to England by now.

Janus was apprehensive about leaving their farm in the hands of three workers from the de Vries estate, but he was also impressed with their work ethic and their knowledge, which did allay his nerves somewhat. However, leaving the farm and knowing they wouldn't be back for a month was still unnerving.

Lenje was totally the opposite: she was excited. It would be the first time she had ever left Frisia. She wondered what England would be like – the food, the culture, the people. All of the de Vries side of the family were rich and well to do, whereas they were just poor farmers.

It took several hours to travel from the farm to the port of Delzijl where they were to meet up with the de Vries and board one of their ships to Hull, sailing on the late evening tide.

The journey was arduous as the road was bumpy and the coach swung from side to side. The horses pulled the carriage at such a quick pace that it made Lenje feel unwell. Janus kept reassuring her that the faster they went the sooner they would arrive. He was not looking forward to the sea crossing.

Arriving at the port of Delzijl, they were met by Maarten and Karen de Vries, Pieter's brother and sister-in-law, who ran the shipping side of the family business.

Pieter and Maritje were already there and staying at his brother's house.

'Welcome, welcome, welcome!' Maarten greeted them when the carriage came to a stop on the dockside.

'I am Maarten, and this is my wife, Karen. We have heard so much about you both from Gionne.'

He held out his hand to help Lenje, who was a bit wobbly, alight from the carriage.

'Please, let's have some refreshments in our humble home before we have to board our ship,' he said. 'Both Pieter and Maritje are here already and waiting for us.'

Inside Maarten and Karen's home, Maritje rushed to embrace Lenje as Pieter shook Janus's hand.

'How was your journey? Comfortable we hope?' asked Pieter as they sat in plush sofas and chairs with tea and a selection of cakes and breads.

Janus explained that they were not used to travelling by coach and apologised for their inexperience. The only time they had experienced a ride in a horse and carriage was for the weekend they spent at the de Vries' Landhuis.

Talk soon turned to the wedding.

'Truus is already at Flintwell Hall helping Gionne and Pim with the organisation.' Maritje said. 'I think she is going to be the Maid of Honour.'

'Apparently, we are all going to be allocated one of the towers in their impressive castle,' Karen de Vries said.

'It's a hall, Karen, not a castle,' interjected Maarten, and everyone laughed.

'It's supposed to be one of the finest houses in England, so Harrietta tells us,' Maritje stated.

'Is Lady Harrietta related to you?' asked Lenje.

'Only by marriage – she is my sister-in-law. Harrietta is Pieter's younger sister. She married Henry Bankes about ten years ago but they don't have any children, despite trying.'

'Does that mean there is no heir to the title and land?' asked Janus.

'I supposed so, but English hereditary law is strange, and they are able to nominate relatives or other branches of the family tree to inherit,' replied Pieter. 'In fact, I believe that Henry has a plan he wishes to discuss with me at the wedding.'

Maarten and Karen's son, Joost, came through the door in a rush.

'The tides on the turn, so we need to make haste. Father, could we get everyone on board? Captain Janssen is getting tetchy.'

Maarten laughed at this. 'I bet he is! Willem is not the most patient of men. But he is a very good skipper,' he added to reassure everyone.

They all filed out of Maarten and Karen's house and Joost led the way to the waiting ship. It was a three-masted square-rigged Fluyt, or Dutch merchant ship, which was lightly fortified against possible pirates. The rear of the ship stood tall on the docks and was beautifully decorated.

The gangplank was quite narrow and only secured to the ship by thick ropes. The gentle swell of the water in the dock meant the gangplank was continually moving, making it a challenge for the ladies in their fine dresses to grip the rope handrail or the strong arm of one of the deck hands.

Joost showed them to their cramped quarters. There were two bunk beds in each and a small table. These passenger quarters were all off the main saloon, where the charts were kept and the captain had his bunk. The saloon at least was fairly spacious and had a large table with seats and a drinks cabinet.

'I suggest we gather on the rear deck near the wheelhouse to watch the departure out of port and then re-group in here for some refreshments.' Maarten wanted them to keep clear of the main deck where the crew would be very busy with ropes and canvas.

'This is the largest merchant vessel we have in our fleet and is normally used on our African and Indian trade routes, so there will be aromas of spice. Pieter asked if we could use her for our voyage to Hull, where she will pick up a cargo and depart for Spain initially.'

Having made sure everyone was settled, Joost said, 'I will leave you in my father's very capable hands as I am required to run the business here whilst he enjoys my cousin's wedding.'

He bade them bon voyage, made his way down the gangplank and stood on the dock to watch the crew and dockhands make preparations to leave.

Two long boats pulled the large ship's bow away from the dock and it slowly began to move towards the open seas with the aid of some of the smaller sails.

Maarten had prayed for good weather and calm seas for a smooth crossing and his wishes, so far, had been granted.

Wrapped in heavy coats and scarves, they all stood at the rear of the ship and admired the disciplined expertise of the crew and officers.

As it left the safe haven of the port, the gentle swell of the sea started to rock the vessel, as the captain pointed the bow to catch the best angle from the wind and fill his sails. The motion was a new experience for most of the guests, except for Karen, who was used to sailing. It gave them their first taste of 'sea legs.' The men stayed on deck whilst the ladies retired to the saloon to take some refreshments.

The voyage would take all night and they would arrive in Hull early the following morning.

A very basic meal was served by the ship's cook: soup and bread with chunks of Dutch cheese and cured ham. It was accompanied by a few bottles of porter and brandy.

'Can I suggest that it's worth wrapping up warmly and watching the sunset from the aft deck?' Maarten said to keep their attention away from the movement of the ship.

On deck there was a fair breeze that filled a full set of sails. The gentle bowing head of the ship as it met movement of water made the ladies hold tight to their husbands and they listened to the noise of the bare feet of the deck hands as they pulled on ropes to alter the sails.

The sunset was astounding, and everyone agreed it was amazing to see this out at sea. The orange ball sunk below the horizon and the night filled with sparkling diamonds under a clear cloudless sky.

It was late in the evening as they all enjoyed a nightcap before retiring to their bunks in an attempt to sleep.

The following morning, they caught sight of the occasional merchant ship and some of the British Naval frigates. Maarten's prayers had been answered as the weather held and the channel crossing was comfortable.

The guests took frequent walks around the decks, enjoying conversations with the crew, who told tales of adventures.

Dawn broke as the big ship entered the Humber estuary. Large mugs of hot coffee and chunks of bread and cheese were handed out to the guests as they stood on the poop deck to watch the arrival into the bustling port of Hull.

Even at this early hour, with the sun barely up, the estuary was busy with many little sailing craft plying the wide expanse of water between both banks. Some were fishing boats; others were ferry boats. There were also several large merchant ships, bigger than the one they were on, with massive three of four masts carrying an enormous amount of sail. These were from either the Americas or the Far East, bound for the major trading port of Hull.

The guests marvelled at the expertise of the helmsman as he navigated their way into port. The crew too were astounding to watch as they used both the sails and their rowing boat to guide their vessel into the allocated dock, folding away the sails and tidying the ropes neatly on deck.

They all waited in the saloon as their travel trunks were taken to the waiting hay wagon sent by the Flintwell Hall Estate.

Also awaiting them were two very fine coaches, doors decorated with the Marquis of Flintwell's crest and furnished with plush comfortable seats. Each was pulled by team of six horses, waiting obediently on the dockside to take them directly to Flintwell Hall and their final destination.

As it was high tide when they arrived, disembarking was easier as the ship rode high above the dockside. With plenty of strong arms to hold onto, the ladies found it easy to traverse the gangplank, though landing on solid ground with their sea legs meant they were still wobbly on their feet.

♦♦♦

Joost was settling down to supper when he heard a commotion out on the dockside.

A troop of six mounted soldiers galloped into the port, headed by a small man on a huge horse. He wore the uniform of a senior ranking officer: gold braid, medals and fancy clothes with black boots splattered with mud.

Joost stood at his door and watched the man point towards the departing ship as it headed out to sea from the secure harbour walls and shout, 'Stop that ship!'

The horses had been ridden hard and were sweaty and jumpy, with alert officers in their saddles, swords drawn as if expecting trouble.

'You there!' the little man shouted at Joost, waving his sword at him. 'I want that ship stopped and returned to the port.'

He dismounted his frisky horse.

Joost laughed.

'That's impossible as we have no way of communicating with the captain,' he replied calmly.

'Well, can't you send a flag signal or sound off one of those cannons?' The man asked arrogantly.

'They are well out at sea by now and nobody will be looking back at the port, nor would the sound of cannon fire reach them now.' Joost wandered over to the odious little man, whom he towered over.

'Why do you want the ship to return to harbour? And who are you anyway to demand such a preposterous and obviously futile order?' Joost looked on amused as the man's red cheeks all but exploded.

'I am Major General Albert Leijtens, Commander of the Dutch Army in this region. I need to follow Pieter de Vries and his party to England.'

He looked up at Joost and added, 'And who the hell are you?'

'I am Joost de Vries, son of Maarten De Vries. Pieter is my uncle – my father's brother – and we own that ship, General.' He couldn't hide his smile.

'It's *Major* General, de Vries,' he spat out. 'My God! Your family are everywhere.' He stomped around the dockside.

'When is the next sailing to Hull?' he asked after a while and in a slightly calmer state.

'Not until next Tuesday, unless you take that ship.' Joost pointed to a smaller coastal trader moored up on the next dock.

'It's due to leave on the high tide, bound for London on its way to Portugal. You could always disembark in London in three days' time and make your way north to Flintshire.'

'That would take over a week, and by that time my quest would be pointless,' Leijtens said angrily.

'Your quest seems pretty pointless anyway,' Joost replied with a grin.

A decorated officer approached the Major General.

'Father,' he began.

The little man spun round on his heels and looked at the officer.

'Commissioner Leijtens, you will refrain from calling me that whilst we are on duty,' he snarled. 'What is it you want to say to me?'

'I am sure Carl will be safe. He'll get word to us when he can.'

'Who is Carl?' Joost asked.

'My nephew. He's in England in pursuit of our quarry,' replied the Major General.

'And who exactly is your quarry?' persisted Joost.

'Why all these questions, de Vries?' he spat back.

'I'm only trying to help,' answered Joost calmly.

'We are after Pim de Vries and his female partner, Gionne van't Kroenraedt. They are wanted for questioning about a series of murders,' replied Hans.

'My cousin? And *Gionne*?' Joost laughed aloud. 'That is preposterous! They could not have committed the vagrant murders – they were in England when the last one occurred.'

'How do you know about that?' The Major General rounded on Joost and came nearly face-to-face with him, or face-to-chest.

'Everyone knows about the vagrant killings, General. It's common knowledge,' Joost replied.

'But how did you know about the latest one?' he persisted.

'A letterman on his way to England came through here and onto one of our traders to Hull. He told us in the tavern over there. Everyone who was there that night heard about it. The murders could not have been committed by my cousin, so why are you in such a rush to get to England?'

'We must stop the wedding taking place,' he answered automatically then stopped in his tracks.

'Why am I talking to you anyway?' he asked.

Joost shrugged, turned and went to finish his supper, closing his door firmly behind him.

Major General Leijtens was fuming at Joost's arrogance and disrespect towards him.

'The de Vries think they own the place,' he muttered.

'They do, Father,' replied Hans under his breath.

'This is futile, back to barracks!' shouted Albert Leijtens, as Hans, standing next to his father's horse, cupped his hands enabling the Major General, with some difficulty, to reach the pommel on the deep saddle and haul himself up onto his horse.

♦♦♦

'I don't want the wedding overshadowed by the threat of this chap Carl Leijtens trying to arrest Pim and Gionne,' Harrietta told her husband at supper. They were dining alone as everyone else was out. Pim and Gionne had gone to stay with Sir Bernard and Lady Louise.

'I will send for Stanley in the morning, together with Blake and Tilley, and agree a plan to lure him out of his hiding place. He has proven to be very resourceful and has used his army training well.'

'You sound impressed, Henry?' she commented.

'Yes, I am and would like to meet him. Pieter always said he was the sensible one in that family.'

'You mean the Leijtens?' Harrietta scoffed.

'You don't approve, darling? He asked.

'Pieter and I were at school with Albert and his two sisters Anneka and Lieke. Rachel DeGroote was also in my class, and she eventually married Albert and produced Hans, their son. Carl is Anneka's son.'

Henry allowed a short period of silence as, knowing his beloved wife, she had more to say.

'Albert was always short, and because of his lack of stature became a bully. His sisters were very friendly and seemed to distance themselves from Albert. Pieter can't stand the man, as he has risen in the army ranks to Major General and now tries to lord it over everyone, thinking he is the most important person in Frisia.'

'But your family, the de Vries, are very prominent in the region. Surely, he must be subservient to Pieter?'

'You would think so, but Albert has little-man syndrome.' She laughed.

James Howell, the head butler, came in with the desserts and port.

'Howell, can you ask Stanley, Blake and Tilley to be in my offices by ten tomorrow. I want to discuss a plan to entice this Dutchman from his hiding place once and for all.'

'Yes, my lord.' Howell bowed and retreated.

♦♦♦

Lord Henry Bankes was standing in the bay window of his office looking out over the rear land, his back to General Stanley, Tobias Tilley, Randulph Blake and Sir Bernard.

'It is imperative that we root out this Dutchman from his hiding place and let the High Sheriff arrest him for trespassing.'

He turned to face them, and they could see how worried he was.

'We cannot have this Dutchman ruin my nephew's wedding. It has been proven without doubt that Pim had nothing to do with these so-called vagrant murders in Frisia. My wife's brother has confirmed that there has been another killing since they both left Holland.' He looked at his closest team of friends and employees.

'Clifford, can you arrange for a party of your best men to scour the woods and lakeside of my land again?'

'And mine that abuts Henry's land?' added Sir Bernard.

'Randulph and Tobias,' Lord Henry was using their Christian names in a rare show of their closeness, 'can you take the gardeners, gamekeepers, stable boys and any staff not helping Lady Harrietta or Mrs Cribbs? Arm them if necessary and search all the edges of my land with Clifford's men.' He paused.

'Let's find this man, Carl Leijtens. But remember, Lieutenant Leijtens is a very well trained and skilful soldier, taught in the art of camouflage and working behind enemy lines, so he will be dangerous. We need to persuade him that he is safe and will come to no harm – the suspicion that brought him here for is no longer valid. Any questions?' he asked.

'I will get my gamekeepers, stable lads and gardeners to join yours Henry,' said Sir Bernard.

'That would be most helpful, Bernard, thank you.'

Everyone shook hands and nodded their heads in agreement.

'Good, I will join you Randulph, if you will get my horse ready.'

The men filed out of Lord Henry's office to gather their men.

Sir Bernard galloped back to his estate to bring his men across. And Clifford Stanley rode hard to organise his men at arms.

♦♦♦

That afternoon more than a hundred men and women swept across the open fields towards the forested boundaries where the Dutchman was thought to be hiding. They were armed with pitchforks, poles, garden forks, swords, scythes and long knives, as well as flintlock rifles.

From the other side of the land, Sir Bernard's men also approached the area.

A troop of thirty mounted officers led by the High Sheriff also joined the hunt for Carl Leijtens.

They invaded the peace and quiet of the countryside with their noisy chatter, verbal abuse of the Dutchman and loud observations on where he could be hiding.

Several men stripped off their clothes and waded into the shallow waters of the lake to inspect the reed bed from the water side.

Hounds barked and howled as they ran through the woods, with men racing after them on foot and on horseback.

They were bound to find him eventually.

♦♦♦

Carl was sitting in a deep hole he had dug on the edge of the woods, in sight of the Hall and the lake. He had made a strong cover that could hold a man if they stood on it.

What he had not reckoned with was the acutely sharp nose of an English bloodhound that stopped abruptly and started stiffing around the area.

'I think Rufus has found something!' he heard the dog handler shout.

A commotion of hooves and feet stamped above and around him, making the edges of his hideaway crumble. He was worried a horse might fall in and onto him.

He had stored his uniform and sword in an old duffle bag he had found in an alcove he had dug out, where he also kept food and a jug of water.

There seemed to be the whole world above him as the excited cacophony filled the still air.

He was afraid they might fire on him, either wounding or killing him. And he desperately tried to remember enough English to stop them from harming him. He expected to be handled roughly – that came with the territory.

Carl looked at the handwritten notes left by Harrietta De Vries or Lady Bankes as she was now and wondered if it were true that Pim was no longer a wanted man.

Either way, it was time to let them find him and to surrender to his fate.

It took them a long time to find the edges of the cover he had expertly made but eventually they lifted it off.

'There you are, you bugger!' a rough bearded gamekeeper shouted at him as Carl stood up, hands in the air.

'I am surrendering. Please no harm to me. I am not armed,' Carl said in broken English.

It took four men to haul him out of the deep hole. One found his duffle bag and threw it up to the man in charge.

'My God, you stink!' said one of the men.

'Please, I speak to Lady Bankes. She knows my language?' he asked.

'We'll see about that. First to the lake with you. You're in need of a bath before anyone meets you, especially her Ladyship,' the bearded gamekeeper said.

They marched him towards the lake and pushed him in.

Randulph Blake sent a messenger to Lady Bankes that they had found the Dutchman and would make him presentable before bringing him up to the Hall.

After a good soaking in the lake, they gave him his uniform to wear and hauled him roughly onto the back of a cart.

Harrietta Bankes, Pim and Gionne were waiting for him in the stable yard. Henry Bankes watched from a window above.

As the cart raced into the yard, Carl jumped off, stood still and saluted.

Harrietta greeted him in their native Dutch: 'Well young Carl, we meet again – in unusual circumstances.'

Carl was relieved at the chance to revert to his mother tongue: 'Lady Bankes! Yes, it's been a while since we met back in Leeuwarden. I am sorry I have been so much trouble. Is it true Uncle Albert has caught the vagrant murderer?' he asked.

Pim suggested that it would be more courteous to those assembled if they were to speak in English and Lady Harrietta assented.

'As long as Carl here understands,' she added.

Carl nodded agreement: 'My English speak is not that good, but I understand more,' he said.

'Carl, no one has been caught as yet, but another vagrant was killed whilst Pim and Gionne were here, so it's not possible for him to be a suspect.'

She paused.

'Did you get the notes we left in some of your hiding places?'

'Yes, I found them but thought it was a trick. I don't remember your handwriting, Harrietta.'

By this time the stable yard was bursting with people wanting to hear what was being said.

Clifford Stanley and Randulph Blake were standing either side of Carl, in case he tried anything.

Sir Bernard appeared with Henry Bankes in the doorway. Henry made an announcement:

'May I thank everyone for their time and effort, especially Sir Bernard and his men. I think we now have the measure of Lieutenant Carl Leijtens, and he will be our guest until we decide what to do with him.' 'So, please return to your duties and there will be an extra coin in your pay for your diligence.'

This went down a treat and all the staff went away happy.

Lady Harrietta turned to her nephew:

'Pim, can you show Carl to the guest room in the east wing, and ask Mrs Cribb to draw him a bath. Perhaps you can find him some of your clothes as you are of a similar size. Mrs Cribb can then clean his uniform.'

'Yes, Aunt,' Pim replied.

'Oh and ask Howell if we can give Carl a hair and beard trim,' she added.

'Carl reverted to Dutch: 'Thank you Lady Harrietta, you are most generous.'

He bowed in respect.

Pim was intrigued by this man and he too slipped back into his mother tongue: 'Come this way, Carl. You must teach me some of your undercover technics, for hunting.'

Harrietta watched them go into the Hall and took Henry's hand. She drew Gionne close to her.

'I am pleased we have a peaceful outcome.' She hesitated before continuing. 'Carl was always a thoughtful, intelligent boy, unlike Albert. He gets it from his mother, Anneke.'

'Indeed, my love,' Henry said squeezing her hand.

'I think Pim and Carl will form a good friendship,' she thought aloud.

♦♦♦

In the trading port of Hull, the two families were made comfortable as possible in the fine coaches, before the horses took the strain and followed each other out of the harbour town and onwards down the bank of the River Humber to the bridge crossing the river at Howden, quite a few miles to the west. Four armed men on horseback escorted the carriages to protect them in case of highwaymen.

At Howden, they crossed a stone bridge and then made haste towards Flintshire following the Roman Road known as the Fosse Way. It would be a good day's travel on rough hard roads, through fields and endless forests.

The journey was arduous and made the ladies feel queasy as the carriage wheels bumped along and the carriages swung on their leather straps. They stopped twice to water the horses, allowing the passengers to stretch their legs, both times outside an inn where they could get food and drink.

The coachman estimated they would arrive after dark, but was confident it would be this evening, as long as there were no highwaymen to disrupt their journey. Each carriage had a coachman, and four armed guardsmen to protect them from such potential encounters, in addition to the outriders on their horses.

Pieter, Maritje, Maarten and Karen took one coach, and were used to such long journeys, so took it in their stride, amusing themselves with games and chatter.

Janus and Lenje however had never experienced such a journey, apart from the one from their home to Delzijl. Alone in the huge coach, they could stretch out on each side of the carriage and sleep in the rocking motion.

At one of the inns, Pieter suggested the ladies travel together for the remainder of the journey, so they could talk about the wedding and the English side of the family. Lenje was very happy to oblige and allowed Karen and Maritje to take her into their confidences. She had a very good understanding of Harrietta and Henry and laughed at some of their childhood tales. Lenje hadn't realised what a close family they were as they were at school together, before Karen and Maritje formed partnerships with the de Vries boys.

Harrietta was destined to greater heights, having met Henry on a guest shoot on one of the de Vries farms. She fell in love with a Lord, soon to become a Marquis, when his father suddenly passed away only months into their marriage.

Janus enjoyed Pieter and Maarten's company, learning more about the de Vries empire. He had no idea how vast it was and how many different industries they were involved in from diamonds to cocoa, farming, and shipping.

Janus was also amazed at how easily he got on with these two great men of power. They treated him like a member of the family and shared all their troubles and opportunities with him on that leg of the journey. He also found out that Pieter, Maarten, Harrietta, Karen and Maritje all went to school together, along with Albert Leijtens.

Shortly before they reached Flintwell Hall, one of the riders was sent ahead to announce the arrival of the coaches.

♦♦♦

An hour later, staff at the hall saw the swinging lanterns from the coaches turn through the gates and on to the private road to Flintwell Hall.

Everyone came out to greet them, even though it was very late in the evening.

The staff headed by Mr Howell, Mrs Pottage and Mrs Cribb stood in a semi-circle behind them, with George Bedlan, the first footman and his team of lads ready to help with any additional bags.

The hay wagon had arrived hours earlier and all their travel trunks and cases had been taken to their rooms.

The coaches came to a halt, the teams of horses stamping their hooves and whinnying after such a long journey. The stable lads took charge to hold the team steady as the passengers alighted the coach on unsteady feet.

The ladies were first to alight, and Gionne rushed forward to embrace her mother, as Pim embraced his own. Truus burst through them all and virtually threw herself at Maritje.

The gentlemen were next out of the second carriage and were greeted by Henry and Harrietta.

'Henry, these are my brothers, Pieter and Maarten, and their wives Maritje and Karen.'

Truus again pushed through everyone to hug her father.

Pim shook Janus's hand and embraced Lenje.

Gionne was laughing and happy as she took her mother and father's hand to introduce them.

'Uncle Henry and Aunt Harrietta, these are my parents, Lenje and Janus,' she said gushing with pride.

'Welcome to our home. Come, we have refreshments for you – and seating – after such a rough ride in our ancient coaches,' Henry announced, as he led the way into the long gallery.

A table had been laid out with food, water and wine, and serving girls stood ready to help.

The Dutch side of the family was overwhelmed by the reception and most grateful for the food and wines.

'Henry, please may I take this opportunity to thank you all for a fantastic reception and your very kind hospitality,' Pieter said in perfect English.

'Think nothing of it, Pieter, after all you are all family!' Henry laughed before adding, 'And I'm afraid your dear sister has not been successful in teaching me any Dutch. I am embarrassed, as your English is perfect.'

'I hope Pim and Truus have been helping you out and not sitting on their backsides?' Pieter said.

'Not at all, in fact quite the opposite: they have taken seamlessly to life at the Hall. We love having them here. And Gionne is an absolute delight, Lenje and Janus; you should be very proud parents.'

'In the morning, we will give you a tour of the estate and bring you up to speed on the wedding arrangements,' Harrietta added.

There was a pause as Henry clinked a fork against his glass to call their attention.

'We have another guest staying with us. He means us no harm and, though he won't join us this evening, we have told him he is welcome to stay for the wedding. Carl Leijtens was sent here by his Uncle Albert to arrest Pim, under the now proven false accusation relating to certain events in Frisia of which you are aware.'

Harrietta rushed to Carl's defence.

'Carl was always the most thoughtful and caring one in that family, so please do not berate him, Pieter and Maarten,' she pleaded. 'His father was Albert's younger brother, married to Anneke, but he was killed in battle ten years ago. Carl had no option but to join military school and Albert made him a lieutenant under his command.'

She paused, sensing scepticism from Pieter in particular, then added, 'If you doubt me, ask Pim. Against all odds, considering what has happened, they've actually become good friends.'

Pieter was not happy, and Harrietta saw this, so took her elder brother away from the gathering to talk sense into him.

They both returned to join the family and Pieter seemed happier.

'It's late, and you have all had a long day, so may I suggest we all retire to bed and get some well needed sleep. Tomorrow, we will give you all a tour of the estate and bring you up to speed on the wedding arrangements,' Harrietta announced.

♦♦♦

Carl had been listening out of sight on the gallery landing that surrounded the long hall. He was relieved that he had supporters and wondered what his uncle Albert had been thinking, placing him in such a dangerous position.

He was still unsure about his safety – especially when it came to Pieter and Maarten. They knew his Uncle Albert and cousin Hans well and there was no love lost between their families. Perhaps his new friendship with Pim would aid in smoothing things over. Harrietta was right: their friendship had been a surprise to them both but they got on famously.

Carl felt uncomfortable with Harrietta's generosity after all the trouble he had caused them. He had however been bowled over by the arrival of Truus, who was not only attractive but bubbly, fun and an accomplished rider as well. They spoke in their native Dutch and he was starting to grow very fond of her.

Yes, he liked her, and he thought there were signs from her too that the feeling was mutual.

♦♦♦

The next morning, and after clearing it with Harrietta, Carl decided to go out for a morning ride, and bumped into Truus and Gionne in the stables saddling up their horses.

He spoke to them both in Dutch: 'Good morning, ladies. We have a similar need for fresh air, I see.'

'Carl, why don't you join us? That is, if you can keep up with two silly girls,' Gionne teased.

They helped him find an appropriate saddle and harness set and a horse from the stable block. Unbeknown to him, the horse was the friskiest in the stables and hardly anyone rode him.

As he mounted, his horse backed up and whinnied then rose on his hind legs. But Carl was an expert horseman and soon had him under control with tight reins.

He noticed the girls were laughing and shook his head.

They trotted out of the stable yard and into the open park before galloping away.

Pim, watched with Harrietta from an upper floor window.

'Do you think it would be strange if I asked Carl to be my best man, Auntie?' Pim asked.

His aunt smiled and shook her head.

'Not at all. I've known the Leijtens all my life and Carl's father was a kind young man, unlike his older brother Albert. There is a lot of his father in Carl. I think he's a fine young man.'

Pim nodded, relieved. Carl had been a revelation to them all.

'Truus is becoming close to him as well,' he observed.

'That can't be a bad match. I would encourage it,' she said, before adding quickly, 'Though I'm not her mother.'

The trio returned an hour later in good spirits.

As they entered the breakfast room, most of the parents were dressed and downstairs.

They burst into the room, giggling and laughing, teasing Carl because they'd beaten him in a race back.

As soon as Carl realised that Pieter and Maarten were looking at him, he approached, bowed and offered his hand, addressing them both in Dutch.

'Meneer de Vries, it's a pleasure to meet you under better circumstances than the last time.' He remembered the tense meeting with his Uncle Albert and Hans at their house in Frisia.

Both Pieter and Maarten stood up and took his proffered hand. Pieter was the first to speak: 'Harrietta has told us that you were sent here by your uncle.'

'Can we all speak in English please? It's rude towards our hosts,' Harrietta reminded them.

'Of course. Apologies Henry. Your Uncle Albert has always been a difficult man, Carl, but I am told you are more like your father,' Pieter said.

Carl nodded. 'I certainly hope so, meneer.' After a beat, he added, 'You were all at the academe together, I understand?'

'Yes, Pieter, Albert and Klaas were in our year,' Maarten replied.

'And Anneke, Lieke, Rachel and Karen were in my year at dame school,' Harriette injected.

'I remember when Klaas and Anneke, first dated, and they were the first to marry. Soon after, you were born,' Pieter said.

'So, we can all blame your father Klaas for starting a wedding trend, as we were married within five years of each other!' Maarten laughed.

'Your dear father was such a loss to your mother. We were sad to hear the news. That bloody war!' Harrietta said.

After a respectful pause, Henry changed the mood: 'Come on, let's all finish breakfast as we have a tour to go on.'

CHAPTER THIRTEEN
The Wedding

'We must have a wedding rehearsal,' the Very Reverend John Portwood announced as they entered the small chapel, set within the grounds of the great park only a short walking distance from Flintwell Hall.

Harrietta was hosting a short tour of the Bankes family chapel.

After introductions, the reverend said, 'I am aware that Gionne and her family are of the Catholic faith.'

'Yes, we are,' Janus said in English.

'You are all most welcome into our humble chapel, where our faith in God transcends all religions. I must inform you that in 1753 the then Lord Chancellor, Lord Hardwick, promoted the Marriage Act, which declared that all marriage ceremonies must be conducted by a minister in a parish church or chapel of the Church of England to be legally binding. He did not offer any guidance towards mixed religions, apart from the requirement from the Church of Rome to give its blessing.' He paused to make sure he still had everyone's attention. 'However, my good friend, Father Lucas Cantonelli, is a Jesuit priest from the local monastery and he has agreed to join me in the wedding ceremony and give his blessing.' Reverend Portwood laughed and added, 'Even though he is Italian.'

'This is very kind of you to think about us,' Lenje said. 'We worried about how their marriage would be seen in the eyes of God.'

'God is all seeing and Gionne and Pim will make a good match,' the reverend assured her. 'Father Cantonelli is fully appraised of your beliefs and those of the de Vries family, and he will give his blessing to a slightly altered yet traditional wedding service.'

The wedding was to be in three days' time and there was a lot to be done before then. Everyone was allocated tasks.

And Harrietta said a silent prayer for good weather.

♦♦♦

'We've found another body, General Stanley. This time on the Fosse Way, a few leagues from Failsworth Hall.'

'Another vagrant?' he asked.

'We believe so. He was on foot and had a large leather travelling bag. Same method. Looks like a fencing sword, looking at the entry wound.'

Clifford Stanley was suddenly aware of the similarity to the vagrant killings in Frisia that sent young lieutenant Carl Leijtens to England to arrest Pim de Vries. He shook his head at the thought; it had to be just coincidence.

'Send a couple of officers to the villages around here to ask for any notable sightings and search the area again, thoroughly. We'll see if anyone saw anything or anyone, particularly anyone on horseback.'

He was faced with a huge dilemma as it was so close to the wedding; anything he did now could have serious consequences.

Maybe he should speak quietly to his Lordship. After all, Henry Bankes was the law around here.

◆◆◆

The activity surrounding Flintwell Hall continued to increase as everyone was gripped by the excitement of the forthcoming event.

The marquee had been erected, tables, chairs and bench seats placed. The food was delivered, and Mrs Pottage was in full swing in the kitchens, preparing as much as possible in advance.

Harrietta took command of one of the morning rooms as her wedding headquarters, and held regular meetings with heads of staff, supervising the build up to the perfect wedding.

Every detail, however small, was rehearsed and reviewed, including the temporary holding of guest carriages and horses in a field outside the great park. Teams of people from surrounding villages were recruited to manage the many horses and carriages they were expecting. Their jobs would include supplying feed for the animals and food for the carriage men.

♦♦♦

The rehearsals were planned for two days before the wedding day, and both families met at the chapel to agree the service, its sequence, and where everyone would sit.

Father Cantonelli joined them for rehearsals. He was a very jovial, rotund priest, dressed in a plain brown cassock and with a bald patch surrounded by dark hair on his head. He spoke softly and slowly with an Italian lilt, which was very endearing.

'Allora, I am so happy to meet you all! Reverend Portwood has been through all the details of this wonderful marriage, and I am more than happy to give you both my blessing.' He stepped forward towards Gionne and drew the sign of the cross on her forehead. She bowed in front of him.

'Thank you, Father,' she said.

Truus stood by Gionne's side.

'And you, young lady must be Truus, the maid of honour?' he asked.

'Yes, I am,' she said.

He drew the sign of the cross on her forehead, too.

'But I am not Catholic, Father,' she said.

'It is of no matter what we all are,' he said, 'as long as we all believe in one God, my child.'

Reverend Portwood stood smiling, noting how Father Cantonelli seemed to magically entrance everyone with his smooth natural manner.

It was clear that Reverend Portwood and Father Cantonelli had the whole service immaculately planned, which gave everyone great confidence.

No one argued with their logic on either the order of service or the seating plan.

Lord and Lady Bankes had their own pews at the front of the chapel but agreed they should give these up for the parents.

As they walked back towards the Hall, Harrietta linked her arm with Gionne's.

'This is going to be perfect,' she smiled.

Truus, linked her arm through Gionne's on her other side and spoke softly in Dutch.

'You are quite right, Auntie. And Gionne is going to be the best sister-in-law I could ever wish for.'

The three of them walked on together.

'I see that the young lieutenant has a soft spot for you,' Gionne whispered just loud enough for Harrietta to hear.

Truus blushed and whispered back.

'He *is* rather handsome.'

'You'll hear no objection from me Truus,' Harrietta said quietly, 'but it may be prudent to speak to your mother.'

Word got around about the fledgling romance and the atmosphere in the Hall that night was electric, with everyone's attention on Truus and Carl Leijtens.

The only one with reservations was Pieter, who knew the family well. The one point in young Carl's favour was that he was nothing like his uncle and everything like his father Klaas.

Carl had been a great help over the last few days in getting involved in the heavy lifting of furniture and other areas of preparation for the wedding. This hadn't escaped Pieter's notice. Nor had the friendship between his son, Pim and Carl. Despite the strangest of starts, the two of them had become thick as thieves. If his son was prepared to forgive Carl so graciously, perhaps he should do the same.

Carl seemed determined to do everything he could to help the families, as if he were repenting his previous actions. It was hard to hold a grudge against him.

♦♦♦

Prior to the big wedding, Flintwell Hall had one bigger event to host: the day of the games.

This was a much-anticipated annual event, held by Lord Bankes, so that everyone in his household could enter the competition after rigorous qualification. All the staff were given the day off to watch on the far side of the field, opposite the family and guest area.

A grandstand was erected on one side of the field with a dining marquee for refreshments, where the kitchen staff who'd volunteered alongside Mrs Pottage could prepare food for all the guests. James Howell and Mrs Cribb were also there to help.

A feast was prepared for the guests with mead, wine and champagne on offer, alongside lemonade and water for the participants.

Food and drink were also provided for the Hall staff in their own marquee with George Bedlan, the first footman, taking charge.

The staff regarded Lord and Lady Bankes as appreciative employers, and the games was the highlight of the year. Every part of the household had their champion, including all the family and retainers of the Bankes.

There would be a contest of fencing, horsemanship skills, and archery.

General Stanley put himself forward to show off his prowess; Lord Corringham's man was his head gamekeeper and, like Stanley, ex-military. Randulph Blake, the estate manager, Tobias Tilly, the gamekeeper, Carl Leijtens and Pim all participated.

There was great amusement when Gionne, urged on by Lady Louise and Lady Harrietta announced her entry. All the men complained that women had never been allowed to enter the games, let alone participate in them.

'What are they all afraid of?' asked Gionne, when Henry Bankes attempted to talk her down. 'Are they frightened of being beaten by a woman?' she scoffed.

In solidarity with her friend, Truus also asked if she could take part, joining Gionne as the second woman of the contest.

Henry Bankes, Bernard Failsworth, Carl and Pim had a heated discussion together with other members of the senior staff.

After several hours of debate, they eventually conceded, Sir Bernard making the point that neither Gionne nor Truus would get past the first round.

Everyone was relieved it was a pleasant, sunny, dry day. Preparations had been taking place in the huge field behind the Hall next to the orchard, where the spectators gathered in excitement. This excitement had increased further once word spread that two women were competing.

Lady Louise and Lady Harrietta watched on gleefully from their huge comfortable chairs on the podium, secretly hoping that Gionne would wipe the smirks off the men's faces. Maritje and Pieter de Vries sat alongside them.

Lenje and Janus were in a state of embarrassment at the thought of their daughter displaying her wild side in front of all these gracious and powerful people. They kept on apologising for her behaviour, though Maritje and Pieter told them not to worry – it would be a great win for Holland if she beat the lot of them. Louise and Harrietta both heartily agreed. They all settled down after snacks and drinks were served.

General Stanley organised his trumpeters to announce the start of the games. Then it was underway.

The first round was horsemanship: the rider had to gather hoops using a lance then place them on a coloured pole – the one who gathered the most hoops in the quickest time won. All the men had their turn and performed well.

Truus tried but was not that confident on horseback, so made an early exit.

Gionne, on Anouk, was the last to ride. Not only did she scoop up all the hoops but rode like a demon and beat all the men's times. She was cock-a-hoop with delight. The staff clapped, shouted encouragement and went wild.

The second event was to race the horse around the field and shoot at a straw target with a bow and arrow – the more arrows on the target the better. Again, Gionne won hands down.

After that event, one or two of the men demonstrated riding bareback – one even rode backwards. Not to be outdone, Gionne stood barefoot and upright on Anouk's back, holding only her reins in one hand – the other in the air – as she cantered around the perimeter of the field. The men were impressed, but also enraged; this was not part of the discipline of the games. They all thought she was showing off but the staff and guests were all thrilled.

The next event was fencing: four bouts of elimination rounds saw the final pair facing each other in the middle of the field. Gionne and Truus had destroyed the ex-military men with their agility and defiance, and now faced each other.

The tension was immense, as everyone knew these two best friends regularly fenced together. Truus fought valiantly but was defeated in the second round by a wild and determined Gionne, who finally stood facing her fiancé, Pim. Everyone was on edge as no one could predict the outcome. These two were known to fence together and were equals.

Stanley officiated in the final bout, signalling to both, they would soon begin.

Gionne stood still, her red hair flowing over her shoulders, her white cotton dress, muddy and torn from her previous events, her brown boots caked in dirt. She smiled at Pim and placed her épée under her arm as she tied a ribbon in her hair to make a ponytail.

'Are you ready for a beating, my love?' she teased.

Pim watched her, knowing this was a tactic to distract him. He resolved to beat her.

With a steely determination and a lightness of speed and agility, Gionne won the first three bouts. It shook Pim, who though impressed by her skills and beauty, was annoyed that he could not win against her.

General Stanley announced Gionne van't Kroenraedt as the overall winner of the games. Gracious in defeat, he presented her with a silver salver and some hastily assembled flowers.

Like Stanley, the men were in awe of her and vowed never to cross her. This would pay dividends for Gionne in the future.

Everyone was astounded by her agility in everything male dominated.

♦♦♦

'Preposterous suggestion Stanley!' Lord Bankes spat out; his face reddened by anger.

They stood in front of his Lordship's desk in his private office, Clifford Stanley, his right-hand man and Carl Leijtens.

Henry Bankes had asked his close friend Sir Bernard to attend the meeting as well.

'So, what you are implying, Stanley, is that there is a great similarity to the so-called vagrant murders that have taken place in Frisia, and since Pim and Gionne have arrived here, there has been a series of similar killings?'

Henry sat back in his chair and looked from Clifford Stanley to Carl.

'What made you so sure it was Pim in the first place, Carl?' Sir Bernard asked.

'My uncle and cousin have been investigating the killings at home and they interviewed everyone in the surrounding villages as well as Leeuwarden.

We also interviewed all the staff and farmers at the de Vries estate. The only person we could not interview was Pim de Vries.'

'And this led you to assume that Pim was responsible for these deaths?' asked Henry Bankes.

Carl looked nervous.

'It seemed a coincidence that Pim evaded our request to speak to him then left to come here to England.'

Carl paused then continued.

'When I arrived here and went undercover, I couldn't see anything that linked Pim to the killings, either in Frisia or here. And there has been another killing in Leeuwarden, I understand, since Pim arrived here.'

'Yes, there has,' Stanley confirmed.

Sir Bernard looked thoughtful.

'Why do you presume that it's Pim and not Gionne that is the perpetrator?' he asked.

Henry jumped to his feet.

'She cannot be involved in this Bernard! How can you even suggest it?'

Bernard shrugged and went on:

'As we have seen, she is an accomplished horsewoman and can beat anyone at fencing, including you Carl,' he said.

Silence fell in the study as each man brooded on this new, if ludicrous, possibility.

'Stanley, tell us what you have discovered so far with your investigation?' Henry broke the silence.

'My men have scoured the area – all the villages and towns – and stopped any travellers. We have nothing to show for it. It's evident that whoever is responsible for the killings is on horseback and uses some kind of thin-bladed sword or épée.'

'Just like the murders in Frisia,' added Carl.

Henry was drumming his fingers on his oak desk.

Carl continued, 'That said, I have spent time with both Gionne and Pim over the last week; I cannot see how either can be a suspect. They have largely been here and nowhere near the place where the last man was killed.'

'Stanley, your men should keep looking. We have to find the killer soon. And we have a wedding to attend tomorrow,' Henry announced, standing up to signal the end of the meeting.

'It's preposterous to even think it could be Pim or Gionne,' he said as his final words.

He took Sir Bernard's elbow and guided him into the next room for drinks.

Carl remained seated and looked at Clifford Stanley.

'What's on your mind, Carl?' he asked.

Carl shook his head then held his hands up to his face.

'I have got to know both Gionne and Pim in the last week. I know for sure it's not them,' he stated flatly. 'Truus has been with Gionne most of the time, rarely leaving her side,' he added.

'Do we know for certain what Pim's movements have been over these last two weeks?' Clifford asked.

'Not for certain, no,' Carl acknowledged. 'But he has been working with me and the servants on preparations for his wedding and has hardly been out.'

Stanley nodded in agreement.

'I can't believe it could be Pim either. So, we will keep searching and hopefully catch whoever is doing this.'

♦♦♦

Sunrise over the forest was spectacular on the morning of the wedding day. It looked like it would be a beautiful sunny day.

Gionne was up very early; she and Truus had hardly slept a wink. They dressed in their riding clothes and headed for the stables for an early gallop around the grounds on Anouk and Pim's horse Viggo, taking Bea with them.

Pim was up early as well. He and Carl had stayed at Failsworth Hall with Sir Bernard and Lady

Louise and were nursing heavy hangovers from the bottles of port they'd finished with Sir Bernard. The three had spent the evening putting the world to rights and attempting to teach Sir Bernard some Dutch.

Breakfast at Failsworth Hall was always a banquet, and Pim was glad of the variety of food they offered to calm the butterflies in his stomach. He was suddenly aware that this exciting day had finally arrived.

Carl walked into the breakfast room looking bright and sprightly.

'Have you no shame, Carl?' Pim teased.

'I don't get what you are saying,' Carl said in broken English.

'He means he has a heavy head from the port you three consumed last night, yet you seem to be fresh as a daisy,' Lady Louise butted in, a wicked smile on her face.

'Oh, that!' Carl said with a shrug. 'I am never affected by alcohol. It was good port though, Sir Bernard. I thank you.'

'You are most welcome, though I hope we can clear our heads before this afternoon's ceremony, eh Pim?'

Sir Bernard gave Pim a light punch on the arm.

'The carriage will collect us at 12 noon to go to the chapel, so make sure you're properly dressed by then, you three,' Lady Louise reminded them.

Back at Flintwell Hall, Janus and Lenje met Pieter and Maritje on the grand staircase, as they went for breakfast.

'Goedemorgen,' Lenje said.

The breakfast room at Flintwell Hall was also a feast, and Lord and Lady Bankes, were already seated.

'Good morning, my friends!' Henry Bankes greeted them. 'Please help yourself to whatever you want. Howell will bring refreshments.'

'We hope you slept well,' Harrietta said in Dutch.

'English please, my dear. Some of us are not as educated as you and proficient in more than one language,' Henry teased.

'I am so sorry, husband, but it is so good to speak in my native language!'

Everyone laughed.

'We are surprised that you have not yet taught Henry some words in Dutch, sister,' Pieter added.

'Ze heft het geprobeerd,' (she has tried) Henry said in a very English accent.

Maritje and Lenje both clapped, praising him.

'Anyone seen the bride or Truus this morning?' Pieter asked.

'They were both dressed and out riding very early,' Harrietta said, just as the girls entered the breakfast room, still in their riding outfits.

'Our ears were burning,' said Truus.

'You were out early. Good ride?' asked Maritje.

'Oh, Mama, we didn't sleep a wink last night, so Gionne and I went to clear our heads. We are too excited!' Truus said.

'I wonder how Pim and Carl got on with Sir Bernard and Lady Louise,' mused Gionne.

'They probably drank Bernard out of all his good port,' remarked Henry with a huff.

They all settled around the huge breakfast table to eat.

'Now, ladies, we will start to get ready by eleven this morning. Mrs Cribb and her team will assist you both. I suggest we all do the same,' Harrietta said, looking at her guests and her husband.

'The carriages will collect us from the main entrance at 1pm for the short journey to the Chapel, unless you prefer to walk, of course. It's not far, and it's a lovely day,' she added.

'We would prefer carriages to the chapel and a walk back after the ceremony,' replied Maritje with Lenje nodding agreement.

'That's sensible, as the bride and groom want to walk back to the wedding breakfast marquee and we can follow them,' Harrietta agreed. 'Our other selected guests will arrive at 1.30 and be escorted to the chapel, with the main entourage arriving at 3pm for the wedding breakfast. There is limited space in the chapel, so it's immediate family only.' Harrietta had already explained this at the rehearsals but felt the need to repeat the plans.

'It's going to be a fabulous day Gionne!' Truus gushed, holding her best friend's hand.

♦♦♦

Pim and Carl walked slowly up the aisle of the little chapel towards the chancel steps and their seats on the right-hand side, admiring all the flowers and decorations. Some members of extended family had already arrived and were seated, though neither knew who they were, so they just nodded or said 'goedemiddag' (good afternoon).

Sir Bernard and Lady Louise stood at the entrance to the chapel to welcome the family guests, before they took their seats on the right side behind the boys, to support Gionne's family.

The little chapel soon filled up.

Pieter, Maritje, and Lenje took the seats allocated to them on the right side as well. Lord and Lady Bankes took their usual seats on the left.

The choir were already in their seats in the chancel. Some were servant maids from the hall, some were boys and girls from the village, and others were farm workers.

The organist started to play some Handel to keep everyone entertained. The ushers periodically walked the aisle to ensure everyone was seated in the correct place.

Tensions gradually rose as they waited for the bridal party.

Pim was rocking from side to side in his fine silk clothes. He kept straining round and looking down the aisle. Carl, cool and resplendent in his army uniform, kept pulling him back by his elbow.

'You are not supposed to see her until Janus gives her hand to you,' chided Carl.

'They are here,' Pim said nervously as the chapel bell chimed 2pm.

There was a commotion outside the entrance as low whispered voices were heard.

The chapel warden signalled the organist and Handel's Wedding March erupted from the organ pipes. The congregation stood and the atmosphere in that little chapel rose to a crescendo as Reverend John Portwood, with Father Cantonelli to his right, signalled to Pim and Carl to step forward,

Pim heard the gasps, the oohs and ahhs, and the light gloved clapping as Gionne and her father walked slowly up the aisle, a flower girl in front, and Truus holding Gionne's short wedding train behind her.

For what seemed an age, Pim held all his nerves to stop looking around and finally turned to see her as Janus stopped just short of the chancel steps.

Gionne was stunning.

Radiant, smiling but with a tear in her eye, she looked at Pim and mouthed,

'I love you.'

Reverend Portwood and Father Cantonelli stood side by side at the chancel steps. Father Cantonelli smiled at Gionne and gave her a wink, which helped her nerves.

The priests waited until the organist had finished.

'Welcome all to this very special and unusual wedding day. Father Cantonelli and I will share the ceremony together. Who gives this bride away?' he asked.

'I do,' answered Janus as he gave Gionne's hand to Pim and stepped back to join Lenje in the front pew.

Father Cantonelli blessed everyone in the chapel, and Reverend Portwood began the service by opening with a hymn.

The choir sang their hearts out and joining them was Lord Henry's deep baritone voice with Lady Harrietta's alto-soprano. Surprisingly, Pieter had a good tenor voice and sang the familiar and popular hymn along with the rest of the congregation.

It was uplifting and joyous.

Both the priests took it in turns to read the psalms, lead prayers and announce the next hymns. Then they both took stages of the wedding itself. Carl fumbled in his uniform pocket to find the rings, causing the congregation to titter.

Reverend Portwood blessed the rings and handed them to Father Cantonelli, who did likewise before handing them to Pim.

It was a magical moment as they shared words of love, faith and obedience, followed by another blessing.

'We, that is Father Cantonelli and I – now both pronounce you man and wife.'

The chapel erupted.

Pieter and Maritje sat next to Janus and Lenje and they all hugged.

'We are now a family,' Maritje said tearfully to Lenje.

Truus took Carl's hand and stood next to him as they all watched the bride and groom. Pim and Gionne kissed for a long time after he had lifted her veil over her head. Eventually, Father Cantonelli coughed loudly to break them up, a huge grin on his round face.

The organist struck up again with vigour as Pim and Gionne walked slowly down the aisle, followed by Truus and Carl and their parents, and the rest of the congregation. Outside, the waiting carriage took them to the marquee at the Hall, so they could greet all the guests. The chapel congregation would walk the short distance back to the Hall.

The wedding breakfast was a feast of local foods cooked expertly by Mrs Pottage and her kitchen staff.

The marquee was packed with local dignitaries and family guests. Harrietta had insisted on erecting a second smaller marquee for all the Hall servants and game keepers who were not involved in the kitchens, serving the guests or clearing dishes after each course. Those working would have their wedding meal when the dancing started.

As the speeches began and Carl was responsible as best man to orchestrate these, he asked Janus to start proceedings. He stood nervously, said a few brief words in broken English followed by Pieter who also stood to toast the bride and groom.

Janus, even though his English had improved over the last month, was still very stilted but gave a good speech about both Pim and Gionne being childhood sweethearts, introduced by Truus.

Finally, Pim rose to thank everyone, especially Henry and Harrietta for their generous hospitality, making Gionne and himself so welcome.

As everyone thought the speeches were over, Lord Henry stood.

A quiet hum of excitement overcame the marquee as everyone anticipated what the Marquis was about to say. This was not planned. Carl stood nervously by.

Lord Henry cleared his throat and tapped a spoon on his wine glass.

'I have something to say, or in truth, to announce,' he started.

'As you are aware, my beautiful Harrietta has been unable to bear us any children, through no fault of hers. Therefore, I had a dilemma in deciding how my lineage would continue. I have no immediate family, cousins or nephews to continue the Bankes line.'

There was a new tension in the warming marquee.

'I have consulted Janus and Pieter, discussed it in the House with my fellow peers and even been to see His Majesty on the matter. You must understand that this is a civil matter that has never in our history been experienced before. We have resolved it legally and His Majesty has given his blessing to my proposal that Pim and Gionne de Vries will inherit our titles of Marquis and Marchioness of Flintshire, through Pim's family connections to my wife Harrietta. He will become Lord Pim de Vries Bankes, and his wife, Lady Gionne de Vries Bankes.'

The room erupted with loud chatter before Lord Bankes asked for quiet.

'As I said, this has never been done before and His Majesty will bestow the titles upon you both at a ceremony at Buckingham Palace soon. We do hope you agree to this?'

Gionne and Pim were speechless and sat in their chairs not knowing how to react.

Lady Harrietta stood and approached them both from behind their chairs and whispered into Pim's ear loud enough so that Gionne could hear as well.

They both stood, bowed to Lord Henry and Pim shook his hand.

'We are speechless, Uncle Henry. All I can say on our behalves, is thank you.'

He glanced across at his parents then at Janus and Lenje – both couples were all smiles.

'If our parents are in agreement, then … yes!'

Lord Henry embraced Pim and then Gionne.

'It is my dearest wish come true. Harrietta and I are so proud to have you as part of our extended family, and I can live the rest of my life knowing our land, our people and the family name will carry on.'

Carl stepped forward.

'Please be standing and toast the new Lord Pim de Vries Bankes VI.'

Everyone stood and repeated the toast.

Then the decibels in the marquee exploded as everyone talked at once.

The Hall staff all gathered at the entrance to the marquee and were grinning and clapping their approval.

Truus came and embraced her brother.

'Does this mean I have to call you Sir Pim or my Lord, big brother?'

'It won't change a thing dearest, sister,' he laughed.

Pieter, Maritje, Janus and Lenje all surrounded Pim and Gionne.

'You all knew about this?' Pim asked.

'We were sworn to secrecy,' Pieter said, adding, 'You know your aunt can be very bossy,' just as Harrietta joined them. They all laughed.

At the back of the marquee, and the only man still sitting at a table, gazing morosely at the bottom of a half-filled pewter of ale was General Clifford Stanley. He was annoyed that his Lordship had not shared this news with him. As High Sheriff of Flintshire, *he* was the legal authority in the county, despite the Marquis being in overall charge.

General Stanley was still mulling over the niggling thought that Pim may be the perpetrator of the recent vagrant murders. Where would it leave him if it were proven Pim had done it? He needed a private meeting with his Lordship very soon.

The band started to play and the floor was cleared for dancing.

CHAPTER FOURTEEN
Several Months Later

Flintwell Hall returned to normal. All the guests had left, the Dutch contingent returning to Frisia, and the grounds repaired from the damage caused by the guests. Life resumed.

Truus and Carl were the only guests who remained and took on duties at the Hall. Truus began tutoring the children in the local school, and Carl joined the gamekeepers in running the estate grounds. He taught them undercover surveillance tactics to stalk deer, foxes and other animals they needed to cull.

Both were in love with each other and would spend a lot of their spare time out riding through the estate or in their rooms in the Hall. Everyone was happy for them, and whispers in the staff quarters were of the next big wedding.

Gionne was grateful her best friend remained, so she spent some quality time with Truus, either riding around the extended grounds or walking and chatting.

Lord Henry took Pim into his study every day to school him on the duties of a peer of the realm and the running of Flintwell Hall and the county of Flintshire. He had a lot to learn before his audience and investiture with His Majesty.

Harrietta took Gionne under her wing and did likewise with her new duties to manage the Hall, as well as her social duties to the villagers under their trust.

So, every night for the two months since their wedding, both Pim and Gionne went to bed exhausted.

One morning, Pim was in Henry's study when James Howell knocked on the door and announced that the High Sheriff needed to speak to His Lordship urgently.

'Please ask him in,' Henry said.

Clifford Stanley rushed into the study but suddenly stopped when he saw Pim was present.

'May I see you in private, your Lordship?' he asked.

'Anything you need to say can be said in front of Pim. After all, he will soon be running the county for me.'

Stanley hesitated and looked very awkward, rubbing his hands together repeatedly.

'Out with it, Stanley,' Henry was getting impatient.

'It is concerning the vagrant killings, Sire.' Stanley hesitated to look at Pim.

'Well, what's happened now? Are you any closer to catching whoever is killing these poor people?'

'Not quite, Sire. There has been another killing on the Fosse Way towards Hull, just outside Flintwell village in fact. A traveller this time. He was killed with a thin bladed weapon through the heart.'

'And you *still* suspect Lord Pim here?' asked Henry.

Stanley shifted from foot to foot in embarrassment.

'When did this happen?' Henry asked.

'In the last week, Sire.'

'Well, that rules out young Pim here, as he has been under my tutelage every day for the last eight weeks. Barely been out of my sight. And the poor lad's not had a chance to go out riding either.'

'Yes, your Lordship. I wasn't suggesting it was Lord Pim,' he said nervously.

'It has to be a highwayman then. Get your troops to stop every letterman and catch any highwaymen.'

Pim could see that Lord Henry was getting annoyed.

'Yes, your Lordship.' Stanley bowed and retired through the open study door, where Howell was waiting to escort him out.

'I'm afraid you will have to deal with that incompetent blithering idiot, Pim,' Henry remarked loud enough for Stanley to hear as he exited.

'Does the High Sheriff honestly think I'm killing these poor people? Like Carl did?' Pim asked.

'It's plain to see you are innocent, Pim, otherwise I would not be passing you my inheritance. Carl realised it as soon as he was thinking straight – it's only his uncle, this Albert chap – who has a fixation with you.'

'I understand now why Clifford Stanley has been so standoffish with me.'

Pim was visibly upset.

'We *all* know you are definitely not the killer, Pim. I wouldn't worry about it. I suspect Stanley is more worried about you being his new boss!'

'We do need to stop these killings though. Carl said that they mirror those back home – the very reason Albert Leijtens sent him over here to arrest me.'

'Harrietta tells me Albert Leijtens is a jumped-up little man with aspirations above his station. He has no jurisdiction here, and I will ensure Stanley gets to the bottom of these killings.' Lord Henry tried to reassure Pim.

'Carl told me there was one more killing after Gionne and I left but nothing since. That seems strange to me.'

'A simple coincidence, I'm sure,' Henry said, signalling an end to the discussion.

♦♦♦

The relationship between Carl and Truus continued to become closer as they spent more time together. Truus accompanied Carl on his inspection of the breeding grounds, the deer parks and other wildlife in the dense woods surrounding the Hall.

Gionne was happy for her best friend. Carl had shown his true character, becoming a crucial member of Uncle Henry's estate team and, perhaps more importantly, a great friend to Pim.

To the onlooker, as lovers, they always seemed close. But Truus held her cards close to her chest, and although outwardly showed love and affection for Carl, inwardly she had a colder heart and a mischievous mind.

She went for rides on her own, sometimes for most of the day. No one knew where she went or if she met anyone outside the estate.

Over time, Carl became suspicious, initially wondering if she had another suitor. But then this suspicion was replaced by something darker: he often saw her riding out through the estate gates alone. One sporting activity she enjoyed was fencing, often sparring with Gionne, Pim or Carl himself, and she excelled with an épée.

Carl was tormented by his new suspicions. On the one hand, he had fallen in love with Truus; on the other, rationally, he could not rule her out as the perpetrator of the vagrant killings.

He could not decide how to resolve his torment.

Should he take this to his Lordship, or to the High Sheriff?

He decided to take more time; to follow Truus and try to catch her in the act and kept his thoughts and suspicions to himself.

♦♦♦

Harrietta received a letter from her brother Pieter, thanking her and Henry for their kind hospitality and to say they all arrived home after a long and rough sea crossing. Life in Frisia was returning to normal, he said.

He also wrote that Albert Leijtens was making a nuisance of himself by rudely questioning Pieter and Janus about Carl and why he had not returned to Holland with Pieter's daughter Truus.

Pieter told the man that it was not his place to inform him of Carl's decision to stay in England. Carl had apparently written to his uncle to resign his commission as an officer, but offered no further explanation, which served to anger the little man further.

There had been no more vagrant killings since the de Vries family went to England and the Major General made accusations once again about Pim, despite Pieter giving him good reasons why he was barking up the wrong tree.

Pieter warned Harrietta that he wouldn't put it past Albert Leijtens to make the journey to Flintwell Hall uninvited.

Harrietta shared her letter with her husband and with Pim, Gionne, Carl and Truus at the breakfast table.

'If the man arrives uninvited, I shall send for Clifford Stanley and he can wait outside on his horse until the High Sheriff arrives,' Lord Bankes announced.

'He is such an obnoxious man, Uncle Henry, that he would barge his way into the Hall and demand to be seen and heard,' Pim warned.

'I will deal with my uncle if he comes, your Lordship,' Carl offered.

'Very well, Carl. Should that happen, I'll leave it to you.' Henry's word was final.

When Henry had left the room, Harrietta sat contemplating the possibilities.

'I will speak with Clifford Stanley and forewarn him. We will not offer your uncle accommodation or invite him to stay, so he will need to take rooms at the tavern,' she said in Dutch.

'I am confused,' Gionne said. 'What would be his purpose in coming here?'

'He has no authority, nor can he make any arrests if the only proof he has is his wild imagination,' Carl added. 'I came to seek out Pim on his orders, but only to persuade Pim to return to Leeuwarden with me. Which was not going to happen.'

They all laughed at this.

'Let me get this straight,' asked Pim, 'Is he coming here, or are we *guessing* he may come?'

'It's only speculation. Your father *thinks* he may come and is warning us to be prepared,' Harrietta said.

Throughout this discussion the only person who made no comment at all was Truus, who listened intensely but said not a word – unusual for her.

◆◆◆

Over the next week, Carl kept a close eye on Truus.

She would ride to the village school and teach her pupils and ride home. When at the Hall, she would help Harrietta or Gionne in their chores or go riding with Gionne around the parkland.

Carl started to think his suspicions were groundless. How could he even think she was a killer?

The following week, Tobias Tilley reported a number of illegally set traps for deer and other animals in the far woods bordering the Failsworth Estate. Carl summoned all the gamekeepers to plan their strategy to entrap the rustlers. For this they had to use Carl's method of undercover hides and wait for the intruders to arrive. They left the Hall and set up their hides surrounding the far woods, anticipating a long wait.

Carl left Tobias in charge and galloped back to the Hall. That night, Henry and Harrietta were hosting a dinner, with Sir Bernard and Lady Louise

Failsworth as some of their special guests. And although he did enjoy their company, he was eager to spend more time alone with Truus.

On returning to the stables at the Hall, Carl noticed that Truus's horse was sweating, as if ridden hard. He looked around the stables at the other horses. Anouk and Viggo were both relaxed and munching on their hay bales.

In the saddle room, Truus's saddle cloth was also warm, the saddle left for the boot boy to clean. Carl looked closer: a trickle of blood, still fresh, adorned the right-side stirrups.

She had been out on her own.

He ran into the Hall, up the main staircase and burst into Truus's rooms without knocking.

Truus was taking a bath and shouted out: 'Who's there? Marie is that you? Gionne?'

Carl didn't answer at first but looked around for her riding clothes. He found the riding boots. The left one had a splash of blood on the bootlace.

'It's me, my love,' he replied.

'Carl!' she replied. 'I wasn't expecting to see you until dinner.'

He could hear the water splashing in the bathtub.

'You can't come in. I'm in my birthday suit!' she giggled.

'Now, I would love to see you in your birthday suit,' he replied in a cheeky voice, whilst quickly searching for her riding breeches.

'Carl, don't you dare come in!' Truus called for her maid, 'Marie, where are you, you stupid girl?'

After a frantic search, Carl found her breeches: a blood-stained tear scarred the left lower leg.

His disappointment was crushing. The girl he loved may not be whom he thought.

The bathroom door suddenly opened, and Truus stood in the doorway wrapped up in a white dressing gown, hands on her hips and wearing a very angry expression.

'How dare you, Carl!' she shouted. 'Bursting into my rooms uninvited and going through my clothes.'

Her face was bright red, enhancing her freckles. An avalanche of russet red hair, still wet, tumbled out of her batch cap and cascaded around her shoulders.

She looked stunning and Carl stood there staring at her with an open mouth.

'Well?' she demanded.

He pulled himself together quickly and picked up her left riding boot.

'Are you hurt?' he asked awkwardly.

She stared at him blankly, looking at her boot in his hand.

'Yes. I was out for a ride and my épée fell out of its scabbard and got stuck in my stirrups. It cut my leg.' She raised her dressing gown and extended her pale bleeding leg.

The wave of relief that washed over Carl almost made him faint.

'Let me call Mrs Cribb and get some medical supplies. We must stop the bleeding and bandage your wound.' His tone and demeanour had changed dramatically.

Truus was overwhelmed by his concern at first, but suspicion soon averted her attention to his excuse.

'Why were you in my dressing room Carl?' she asked warily.

He hesitated for the briefest of moments.

'I was putting my saddle in the boot room for cleaning and saw yours there with blood on the stirrups. I was very concerned you might be injured so I rushed up to see you,' he said plausibly.

Marie walked into Truus's dressing room carrying the medical box.

'Oh, I see. Well, thank you. I am fine and now Marie is back, we can patch this up. I will see you tonight.'

He was dismissed.

♦♦♦

At 7pm, Carl stood at the bottom of the grand staircase waiting nervously for Truus. Would she still be angry with him?

He heard voices and movement from the top of the landing and looked up. Truus looked stunning. She was dressed in a long cream silk ball gown, with silk slipper shoes and a tiara in her red hair, which was tied up elegantly on top of her head, exposing her pale skin and elegant long neck.

His eyes never left hers as she walked slowly down the wide staircase. She smiled at him and took his arm with a gentle squeeze. He felt as if she had forgiven him.

'You look sensational, Truus,' he whispered in her ear as they walked into the grand dining room and joined the other guests.

He watched her as she greeted Gionne and Harrietta with warm kisses on each cheek, and then punched her brother who was standing next to them as he made a rude remark in Dutch.

Lord Henry coughed his disapproval of their speaking in Dutch.

Carl's fleeting suspicion of Truus melted away and he fell more in love with her.

♦♦♦

Over supper the discussions turned to the vagrant murders and how frustrated the High Sheriff and his Lordship were becoming. They felt vexed that after all the man hours spent interviewing what seemed like the entire county, including every villager, and the investigation by the Sheriff's men, they had produced not a scrap of evidence as to who the perpetrator was. Carl had been a major contributor to the effort as he was well acquainted with the murders in Frisia.

It occurred to Carl that his sole reason for coming to England had been to apprehend Pim – the key suspect – and bring him back to Frisia. He was suddenly amused at the outcome – especially finding true love with Truus. A hunt for a murderer had somehow morphed into love.

As the conversation progressed in detail, Truus sat very quietly picking at her food. Carl noticed that she did not contribute to the discussion but was alert and listening to every word.

CHAPTER FIFTEEN
200 years on – 1975

Work to clear the far woods had begun, as part of the sale agreement from Lord Henry Bankes, the 9th Marquis of Flintshire.

Death duties from his father's recent demise after a long illness had forced the young Earl to sell some land, which he was clearly unhappy about. The land in question was a treasured area of historic value – it was the site of the original chapel from the 1700s and contained family graves that had to be moved to the new estate chapel near the Hall.

The land was acquired by a developer who planned to build luxury houses surrounded by lakes and a golf course. The plans required that the ruins of the de-consecrated chapel be dug up and the little woods surrounding it cut down.

Henry Bankes was very anxious; he knew from family history events that occurred in the late 1750s drew a veil of mystery and shadow over the Bankes family good name.

His ancestral grandfather, Pim de Vries, married Gionne van't Kroenraedt. Pim – on the death of Henry Bankes the 5th Marquis, – inherited the title with the authority and blessing of the king, as was the late marquis's bequest.

Lady Harrietta, Pim's aunt, lived a long and happy life, guiding the two young people through their responsibilities on running the estate.

Pim's sister Truus had married Carl Leijtens, who both had senior roles in managing the Hall and estate. Truus and Gionne became even closer as the years went by.

Although Henry's relatives were buried in the family vault near the Hall, Truus and Carl were buried in the old chapel cemetery with other senior members of the household. No one really knew why. The only clue was some old family documents referring to Truus's possible mental illness – meaning some form of dementia or psychosis.

♦♦♦

'Sorry to interrupt, your Lordship.'

The foreman of the demolition team had knocked on Henry's study door and entered as was customary.

'That's fine, please come in and take a seat,' he beckoned.

'I'm afraid we've hit a snag on excavating the old graves.'

'Oh? What sort of snag?'

'Amongst the graves there is a very large stone tomb and inside is a very sturdy oak coffin of a relative of yours, sir.'

A chill passed through Henry.

'Who is it?'

'Truus Leijtens.'

Henry knew the name immediately from hours spent looking into his ancestry and the history of the Hall. Truus was Pim de Vries Bankes' sister and married to Carl Leijtens, part of the senior household in the 1750s.

'I see,' Henry said. 'Why is this a problem? Can we not move the tomb to the new family cemetery?'

'We tried but it collapsed and the coffin sprung open. We found this small casket inside next to the remains.'

He handed the Marquis a small ornate silver box. The hinges were very stiff and rusted with age and Henry requested some oil to ease them open. It took some time to open the lid. Inside was a piece of parchment. It was a sealed note, written in Truus's own neat handwriting.

1795 Flintwell Hall, Flintshire

My name is Truus de Vries. I am married to Carl Leijtens.

This is my confession.

Ever since I was young, I was fascinated by death. My brother Pim taught me to ride, to shoot and to fence. My best friend at school was Gionne van't Kroenraedt.

Gionne and I have always been very close, and I must admit I was jealous at first of her close friendship with my brother and then they fell in love.

However, I met a wonderful man in Carl Leijtens, whom I eventually married and loved dearly.

In my last years living in Frisia, I took pleasure in venting my jealousy by killing vagrants – useless people. I would ride at them and use my épée to pierce their heart. It took skill to target the point at the right place to kill instantly so they felt no pain. I practised this on old dead trees in the woods surrounding my home in Frisia and here in England.

I found it amusing that the horrible little man, Major General Albert Leijtens and his son Hans, could not find me, despite me being right under their noses.

My adorable husband Carl – Albert's nephew – is entirely innocent of my crimes or indeed any knowledge of them.

When Gionne and Pim announced they were to marry, I was invited to go over and help with the wedding preparations. I of course, readily accepted.

This is how I came to Flintwell Hall and to the lovely family, the Bankes. I was welcomed with open arms.

Life was marvellous, and I gave my heart to Carl, who had been sent by his horrible uncle to apprehend Pim.

Regrettably, my thirst for cleansing the land of vagrants returned.

Although the authorities and my Carl have spent many years searching for the perpetrator, I was never seriously considered a suspect, though Carl had a brief suspicion at one time, following me on rides and asking questions about my whereabouts.

The burden of guilt has been great and I cannot continue with this charade. I have therefore decided to end my life before my actions bring shame on this wonderful family and my husband.

So, this is my confession:

I am the vagrant murderer of Frisia and Flintshire.

All I ask is not to be buried in the family grave, but in the servants' chapel on the hill.

My love to you all – my brother Pim, sister Gionne and my darling husband Carl.

Think not badly of me.

Truus.

Henry reread the letter several times in disbelief. He knew of this strange period of family history, but not that the killer had been in their midst all along.

'Thank you. Can you let me have time to think about the tomb and grave, and work around it?'

'Of course, your Lordship. There is also another tomb – that of Carl Leijtens – next to this one.'

Henry had to adhere to protocol given that Truus was a family member but also a murderer. Could she be interned in the family graveyard? He needed advice.

He was sitting, deep in contemplation, holding the little silver box when his wife walked in.

'What is that?' she asked, sitting next to him.

He handed her the box and the letter.

After reading it twice, she gasped.

'My god! This does throw light on your ancestor's behaviour and explains the gaps in your history.'

'My problem is that the contractors want to move the tombs to the family graveyard, and I don't know what the right protocol is,' he said glumly.

'Ask Gerald – he knows everything.'

♦♦♦

They all gathered in the small family graveyard: Henry, Bianca, the contractor, the developer, and Gerald, their solicitor, who was holding a map.

'I see no reason why they can't be moved to this area here.' He was standing at the far end of the graveyard near the stonewall border.

'You can reconstruct her tomb and place the other next to hers. She will be a respectful distance from your ancestors, and it will be a while until the space between them is filled,' he said bluntly.

'Yes, I can see that.' Henry nodded. 'So, it is then,' he agreed.

'My Lord, may I suggest that Truus's confession and the silver box be placed in the family vault along with the other historical documents,' Gerald said coldly.

'It may also be wise to inform the Lord Chief Justice, Baron Judge. He will require a copy of the confession and may also have to inform the Dutch Justice as well; it may be centuries old but it's still an unresolved case.

Henry was reticent: 'Will this not bring shame on my family and raise media hysteria?'

'Not if Your Lordship speaks directly to Baron Judge and convinces him that as this was 200 years ago, it should be quietly filed away.'

♦♦♦

On the day the tombs were moved, along with the coffins and remains of Truus and Carl, the sky grew grey and dark. As the day progressed, the temperature dropped to a cold dampness; the wind picked up and, through blackening clouds, a torrential storm began to rage, soaking the men working on rebuilding the tombs and transferring the coffins.

Henry Bankes stood gazing out of his study window, watching the storm build, as if it was the wrath of Truus de Vries.

Was this going to be the legacy he and his future family would live with? His ancestral grandfather Pim de Vries would have been horrified had he known it was his sister who had a wild murderous streak within.

As the storm built itself into a fury, a determination grew within Henry and a plan began to form. No! He would not allow cruelty and violence to define his family legacy. He knew the senseless murders; the bloodshed and the deception had occurred centuries ago but that didn't mean amends could not be made. And he would be the one to make them. Henry resolved there and then to find means of repenting for his ancestor's sins.

All that evening, he watched the storm rage from his window. As it grew in strength, his determination swelled, his resolve hardened and a plan took shape.

By midnight, his kernel of an idea was fully formed and he took it to his wife, Bianca. The two of them stayed up all night discussing possibilities and fine-tuning the details.

By morning they had something solid and achievable. Henry put in a call to Gerald and the hard work began.

***

One year later, a newly adapted Flintwell Hall opened its doors to a new kind of guest. Then another. And another.

The grand gates stood open and a modern looking sign graced the stone gatepost:

Flintwell Hall

A safe haven for the lost and the lonely.

Welcome.

Restitution

Henry passed away in 2015 after a short illness but in the preceding forty years, with the help of Bianca and his trusted team, had transformed his brainchild – the Bankes Trust – into a growing and successful charity. Flintwell Hall, the ancient family pile, still looked much the same on first glance, but had been converted from a private home into a shelter for the homeless. Palatial bedrooms had been refitted and turned into dormitories, and the stables turned into workshops for the residents to learn and refine new skills.

The old kitchens still provided meals three times a day, but instead of serving the landed gentry, they served the vulnerable.

Henry considered it his greatest achievement and derived huge pleasure from taking meals to the residents. He often wondered what his ancestors would think: lord of the manor acting as a servant. The thought made him smile and the act filled him with joy. It gave him purpose.

Truus's heartless words about those she'd killed frequently floated back to him: 'useless people,' she'd called them. Henry's anger at her cruelty and lack of compassion fired his desire to make amends.

By the time of his death, the Bankes Trust had helped more than three thousand individuals. Going forward, and now in the capable hands of Bianca and a committed team, the Trust intended to offer accommodation, support and education for tens of thousands more. Henry Bankes had defined his legacy.

He was buried in the family chapel, alongside his ancestors, and visitors often commented on the aura of serenity that seemed to surround his grave. The inscription on the gravestone was a direct rebuttal to Truus and a reminder of Henry's belief in humanity:

> **Everyone in this world has a purpose. You just have to find it.**

The End

Thank You!

Thanks for reading my book.

If you loved this book and have a moment to spare, I would really appreciate a short review on *Amazon.com/ Kindle* or my Facebook page: *www.facebook.com/chrisdaleauthor.*

Your help in spreading the word is gratefully received and very much appreciated.

You can also stay up to date with my other books, by subscribing to my mailing list on: www.chrisdale.info/contact

or e-mail me at: chris@chrisdale.info

ABOUT THE AUTHOR

Chris Dale was born in 1954 in Lima, Peru. He came to the UK in 1964 for a private school education, spent five years in Cheltenham, and finished his education in France. He built his life skill experiences through a varied career in aviation, the travel business, and then in brand management in the food and brewery markets through the retail food industry. In 2004, he set up his own management consultancy business working in these markets, specialising in launching and managing several different premium brand products. At the same time, as an aviation nut and private pilot himself, he set up The POM Flying Club at Humberside Airport, which he still owns and runs today.

In July 2014, Chris suffered a major stroke that forced an early semi-retirement from the business world, and a total change of direction. The upside of the stroke has created his joy of writing books.

He now spends his time writing and managing his books as an indie author, managing his beloved flying school as a hobby, and doing some voluntary work locally.

This book will be his final novel, as he was diagnosed with mixed dementia in January 2024, hence the difficulties he has had trying to remember the storyline, and the reason why it has taken so long to write. 'I am hoping we will be able to get this published through Amazon books and Kindle, so that it's out there for friends, family and the public to read.'

Also, by Chris Dale

Semi-autobiographies:

My Stroke …. "just get on with it …."
The Boy from Peru

Mysteries:
The Magic Christmas Table
The 14:52

Romantic thrillers:
Crimson Love
The 42 Million
The Bentley Regatta
The Chameleon Pilot
When Her Head Hits the Pillow
The Ghosts of Rodewelle Hall
Two Meters Apart
Papi
Deceived
The Confused Pheasant

www.chrisdale.info